THE RETURN OF
THE MILDEW GANG

Borgo Press Books by S. Fowler Wright

Arresting Delia: An Inspector Cleveland Classic Crime Novel
The Attic Murder: An Inspector Combridge & Mr. Jellipot Classic Crime Novel
The Bell Street Murders: An Inspector Combridge & Mr. Jellipot Classic Crime Novel
Beyond the Rim: A Lost Race Fantasy
Black Widow: A Classic Crime Novel
The Capone Caper: Mr. Jellipot vs. the King of Crime: A Classic Crime Novel
Crime & Co.: An Inspector Cleveland Classic Crime Novel
Dawn: A Novel of Global Warming
Dead by Saturday: An Inspector Cleveland Classic Crime Novel
Dream; or, The Simian Maid: A Fantasy of Prehistory (Marguerite Cranleigh #1)
Elfwin: An Historical Novel
The End of the Mildew Gang: An Inspector Cauldron Classic Crime Novel (Mildew Gang #3)
Four Callers in Razor Street: An Inspector Combridge & Mr. Jellipot Classic Crime Novel
The Hanging of Constance Hillier: An Inspector Cleveland Classic Crime Novel
The Hidden Tribe: A Lost Race Fantasy
The Jordans Murder: An Inspector Combridge & Mr. Jellipot Classic Crime Novel
The King Against Anne Bickerton: A Classic Crime Novel
The Mildew Gang: An Inspector Cauldron Classic Crime Novel (Mildew Gang #1)
Murder in Bethnal Square: An Inspector Combridge & Mr. Jellipot Classic Crime Novel
The Police and the Public: Some Thoughts on the British System of Justice
Post-Mortem Evidence: An Inspector Combridge & Mr. Jellipot Classic Crime Novel
The Return of the Mildew Gang: An Inspector Cauldron Classic Crime Novel (Mildew Gang #2)
The Rissole Mystery: An Inspector Combridge & Mr. Jellipot Classic Crime Novel
The Screaming Lake: A Lost Race Fantasy
The Secret of the Screen: An Inspector Combridge & Mr. Jellipot Classic Crime Novel
Spiders' War: A Novel of the Far Future (Marguerite Cranleigh #3)
Three Witnesses: A Classic Crime Novel
Too Much for Mr. Jellipot: An Inspector Combridge & Mr. Jellipot Classic Crime Novel
The Vengeance of Gwa: A Fantasy of Prehistory (Marguerite Cranleigh #2)
Was Murder Done? A Classic Crime Novel
Who Murdered Reynard? A Classic Crime Novel
The Wills of Jane Kanwhistle: An Inspector Combridge & Mr. Jellipot Classic Crime Novel
With Cause Enough?: An Inspector Combridge & Mr. Jellipot Classic Crime Novel

THE RETURN OF THE MILDEW GANG

BEING THE SECOND VOLUME IN THE MILDEW GANG TRILOGY

An Inspector Cauldron Classic Crime Novel

by

S. FOWLER WRIGHT

WRITING AS "SYDNEY FOWLER"

THE BORGO PRESS

An Imprint of Wildside Press LLC

MMIX

CONTENTS

CHAPTER I.

A Council of War at a Quiet Spot

EUSTACE LIMBROOK and Billie Wingrove (who was his half-sister, a girl of twenty, seven years younger than he) sat together in the old-fashioned parlour of a village inn on the west coast of Scotland. The open window looked out on a quiet, wind-rippled bay, now reddened with sunset light. They had the appetites of healthy youth in a keen air; and an abundant meal, with the added excellence of wholesome simplicity, was spread out between them.

Their relationship was one which will often fail to reveal itself in any similarity of features, and a stranger who saw them together there might have thought them to be lovers rather than united by bonds of blood.

It was a scene of holiday peace, and even the fishing boats drawn up on the pebbly beach had an appearance, as they lay somewhat over upon their sides, of having abandoned toil to drowse on memories of more strenuous days.

But peace was not the emotion dominant in Billie Wingrove's heart; and though it was no more than three hours since they had arrived from Oban (after flying from Croydon in the early hours of the day) with enough luggage to suggest that they had come for a holiday of unusual length, her thoughts were already upon the quickest way by which they could return to London without coming under the observation of those whom they had no reason to call their friends.

A few weeks before Billie had had no cause to think that anything more momentous than the loss or gain of one of the patrons who kept her busy in research work at the British Museum would be likely to disturb the serenity of her life; and Eustace, a civil engineer returning home from Egypt, where he had lost his appointment through the bankruptcy of the firm he served, had thought that the hazard of obtaining a new position in his precarious profession was cause for as much anxiety as any man would find it tolerable to have.

But since then he had been, however innocently, involved in the smuggling of noxious drugs, he had been arrested for a murder with which he was not concerned, and both Billie and he had assisted the police, at no light risk to themselves, in what now looked like an abortive effort to obtain evidence of criminal practices against the heads of the Mildew Gang.

In the end, the police had hurried them out of London, as people whose use to them was ended, and for whose safety they were concerned; and the only tangible results of three exciting weeks were a cheque for two thousand pounds, nominally for false imprisonment and actually for services to the police, which was in Eustace's pocketbook, still uncashed, and a hundred one-pound notes, earned by Billie in a less legal manner, of which over ninety were still unspent—these, and a Whitechapel address which she memorized since it had been whispered to her by Mr. Catsgill, the solicitor who now lay between life and death in a London hospital, a victim of those who had feared (not without cause) that he would betray them to the police.

It was that address, known to herself alone, and now confided to Eustace, which had determined her that she must return to London, if possible while it would still be supposed that they were making holiday on the Scottish coast.

Now Eustace looked speculatively at the girl whom he had promised his mother, when he had been no more than a boy of twelve who would be orphaned on the next day, that he would always care for. He had kept his word. There had been no failure in that. And there was a degree of love and understanding between them now which those of a still closer parentage do not always feel. But, even so, force of character will prevail, and Billie was not easy to guide, and could not be ruled.

"Don't you think," he asked, "we might leave matters to the police now? After all, it's their job. And they've shown that they don't need any more help from us by the way they've dumped us here."

"They wouldn't have done that if they'd known about the address Mr. Catsgill gave me."

"Which may be useless. On his own statement it was two years old, if not more."

"He couldn't have looked at it that way."

"No. But he may have been wrong. Suppose we stay a few days, anyway? We should be far more likely to get back to London without being noticed if we do that. And it will give the police a chance to clear matters up their own way."

"You know they'll do precisely nothing. They've decided that the evidence isn't strong enough to make any more arrests now, and they just mean to lie low."

"Well, they ought to be the best judges of that. And, after all, you say that Catsgill told you not to use that address while he was alive."

"Not exactly. He told me not to give it to the police while he was alive. He must have thought that, if I did, Mildew'd know it had come from him, and that he was giving the gang away. But they must have got suspicious without that, and now they've nearly killed him he won't be safe, if he doesn't die in the hospital, many hours after he gets out.

"He couldn't have thought of things happening just as they have. But I'm not meaning to tell the police. I'm going—we're going, that is—to find out what we can, and, if it's nothing, neither they nor anyone else need ever know. But if we get any evidence on which the police can act, they might arrest Mildew at once, and I suppose that would make Mr. Catsgill safe; and I don't know what else would."

"What it means is that you're to—we're to risk our lives to make Mr. Catsgill safe—and he may be already dying! You can't expect me to be enthusiastic over you doing that."

"I thought we'd gone over all this in the plane! But you know it isn't only for Mr. Catsgill. It's to break up a drug-trafficking gang that does more harm than all the murderers that were ever hanged. That's what Inspector Cauldron said, and the police ought to know. And of course you needn't do anything. I might be safer going alone."

"Don't be silly."

"But the fact is, Eustace, it's all humbug talking about noble motives. I may have some. I don't see how anyone could find that out when I'm not sure myself. But I *like doing it*. That's the honest truth. And I don't want to leave this thing till it's all cleared up. Not if I have to borrow your pants and get a place in the C.I.D."

"I believe there's a medical examination, which you might find to be an awkward preliminary to get over."

"I expect there is. There's always some beastly obstacle when a girl wants to do anything. But I might find some way of getting over that. Inspector Cauldron might help. He'd do anything for me. I dare say you noticed that. Only he thought I was certain to marry you, and that rather cramped his style. It's wonderful what detectives aren't able to see."

The firm lines of Billie's mouth softened into a dimpling smile, and there was a light of laughter in her grey eyes, at recollections she did not propose to share in a more detailed candour.

It was a revelation to Eustace of something he had had no cause to suspect, and little opportunity to observe.

"I hope," he said, "that you're not thinking of marrying that man."

"Oh, he's not so bad! But as to marrying him—do you know he laid a pair of dirty shoes on a chiffon dress that I'd only bought two days before? Fancy marrying a policeman who couldn't detect the dirt on his wife's shoes! No, I think not. I couldn't do with him less than three doors away."

"Well, I hope you won't. Though I don't suppose it's a matter on which you'd listen to me. But there's one thing certain. We can't leave tomorrow till the London papers arrive and we see what Cauldron has put in them about our coming away."

"I should say he's married us, more likely than not."

"Even a policeman wouldn't be such a fool as that."

"Oh, you never know! The London police are wonderful. Aren't Americans mainly occupied in telling us that...? But suppose we go a stroll before it gets darker than it is now? There's one advantage of a quiet place like this, that if we're conspicuous, other strangers would be the same."

"We needn't worry about that tonight. If Mildew means to have us followed, which isn't likely at all, they couldn't be here now unless they had flown, as we know they didn't. He probably won't have any idea we've left London at all till he sees it in the papers tomorrow morning."

"Oh, I'm not worrying about anything! I'm only dying to get out while we can see further than across the road."

Eustace saw that that was literally true. She was not in a mood to worry, or for any counsels of prudence to be received. She was experiencing some reaction from the strains of the last three weeks, beneath which the spirit of new adventure stirred.

The most he could do that night was to obtain agreement that they would not return to London until the metropolitan morning papers had arrived, which, in that remote village, could not be until late in the day; and even that concession was, as he recognized, a tribute to feminine curiosity rather than prudence or his persuasive powers.

CHAPTER II.

THE PRICE OF NOTORIETY

THE morning brings counsel. That is a proverbial wisdom. Billie Wingrove woke happily from a night of untroubled sleep to see sunshine falling on a white bed, and to be aware of the scent of hydrangea bloom through the open window, and the salt breath of the sea. She was carefree still, but in a more sober and practical mood than the night before.

When they met at breakfast she readily followed Eustace's lead, as he encouraged her in discursive talk, and it was not until her spoon was deep in her second egg that she reverted to the argument of the previous night by saying: "I've been thinking that it mayn't be easy to get back to London without being noticed.... Of course, a good deal will depend upon what the police have let out to the Press."

"Yes. I've been thinking of that, too. The more they emphasize that we've come away from London, the more they call the attention of people round here to whom we are."

"Of course, they won't say anything about the Mildew matter. They'll leave him to work that out for himself. They can't say more than that they made a ghastly mistake in arresting you for murdering that Houghton woman, and that you've come here to get as far away as possible, now they've owned up to being the fools they were."

"They won't put it quite like that."

"No. Perhaps not. But it will boil down to that. And the trouble is that it's the Houghton matter which will make people curious. There aren't many people arrested for murders they didn't do, and who say: 'Well, have it your own way. Call me any name you like, and say I did what you please!'"

"I didn't say exactly that. And it isn't that which interests people as much as the way Miss Bingham proposed to identify me."

"Well, anyway, there it is! And until we see the papers we can't tell exactly what soup we're in."

But, in fact, they did not have to await the arrival of the London papers to appreciate the consequences of such publicity as Eustace had unwillingly gained, for they had scarcely concluded the midday meal, for which they returned to the inn with lively appetites after a morning upon the cliffs, when they heard the clanging of the iron bell in the hall, by which visitors to the Prince's Head made their presence known, and were informed that Mr. Alec Mackintosh of the *Glasgow Standard* desired to see them.

Mr. Mackintosh was a lanky, sandy-haired youth with earnest eyes in a much-freckled face. His Scottish accent was unconquerably strong, but his English rarely lapsed from careful correctness. Sent by his editor to Oban that morning, armed with a camera and a cutting from the *Daily Telegraph*, he had proved his fitness for his chosen profession by the celerity with which he had traced his quarry, his means of transit having been the motorcycle which now leant against the wall of the inn.

"I thought," he said, diplomatically tendering rather than asking for information, "you might like to see this." He offered Eustace the newspaper cutting.

Eustace read that which he already knew, and was equally interested to observe what was not there. His arrest, under an identification that must have been deliberately false, was stated frankly enough. It was a blunder for which the police had some excuse, and which could be the more readily admitted now that the true Houghton had been traced, and the woman who had misled them had been detained on the high seas and would soon be in the custody of the French police. Mr. Limbrook, it concluded, had flown to Oban yesterday, in company with his sister, Miss Wingrove, to recuperate from the unfortunate experience through which he had passed. If it were true that Inspector Cauldron had been ignorant of the relationship between them, it was evident that someone at Scotland Yard had been better informed. There was, of course, no mention of the Mildew Gang.

"It was," Eustace said politely, "extremely kind of you to go to so much trouble to bring us this."

Mr. Mackintosh gazed at him with unsmiling seriousness. It was evident that a sense of humour would not obstruct the success of his chosen career. "I hoped," he said, "that you'd let me take one or two pictures and give me something that I could use—and it's grateful I'd be if you were out when the other boys come along."

"You think there'll be other reporters looking us up?"

"Yes, there'll be that."

"I don't want to refuse, after you've come so far. I don't see why you shouldn't take some snaps if you think they'll be any good to you. But I've really got nothing to say beyond what's printed there."

Mr. Mackintosh was unconcerned. "There's a good story behind that," he said; "and if you'll tell it, we won't print anything that you don't want."

Eustace saw that capitulation might be wise. In answer to questions of a competent directness, he gave facts. They related only to his supposed connection with the Houghton murder, and the reporter was unlikely to ask about that of which he was unsuspicious, and concerning which nothing had become public. It was apparent that the interview would tend to persuade any better-informed reader that Eustace knew or cared little about the separate criminalities in which he had been so nearly involved.

The mere fact that he had given the interview, and allowed pictures to be taken, would support the view that both Billie and he had nothing to fear. The police could not be requiring their assistance for any evidence they could give against the Mildew Gang, or they would have kept them in London. They themselves could have no fear that the enmity of the gang would be directed against them, or they surely would have been less careless to allow public knowledge of where they were! What could be better than that?

Mr. Mackintosh took the photographs. He read over his notes with concentrated earnestness. He had one further question to ask: "You'll he claiming compensation for this? It's false imprisonment, whatever excuse the police had about being misled. That doesn't let them out."

Eustace remembered the conditions under which he had received the still uncashed cheque for two thousand pounds from the Home Secretary's office. He replied with pardonable obliquity: "Oh, I don't know that they were so much to blame! I didn't act very wisely myself. It was an unusual position to be in. But I'd rather you didn't publish that I've said that. I'd rather that nothing about compensation should be said at all."

Mr. Mackintosh promised. But he made a condition. He wished to be sure that no other reporter would be able to print anything on a matter omitted by him. That gave Billie an opportunity for which she had been watching. "They'll have to be here quickly, or they won't see us at all. We're not staying after tonight."

Mr. Mackintosh looked interested. Eustace concealed surprise at a seeming indiscretion which it would be useless to contradict.

"I thought," the reporter said, "you'd come here for a long holiday."

"We've come to Scotland for a long holiday, but we don't mean to stay all the time in one place. It's to be more like a walking tour."

Mr. Mackintosh saw no cause for surprise in that, but he made a further note. Billie suggested that he might like some tea before going. With some persuasion he stayed.

As she poured out the cups, she began enquiries as to the best direction in which they might go. Mr. Mackintosh could doubtless tell them much of beauties to be explored, of ways to avoid? He responded readily. For the next half hour she interviewed him, gaining much interesting knowledge, and—which was her more immediate aim—impressing the reporter's mind with the reality of the programme she had announced

In discussing routes it was natural that the question should arise of what time they had free. Billie was frank on that. Perhaps three weeks. Perhaps four. After that Mr. Limbrook might or might not return to London. That was for him to say. But she had research work to take up which could not be longer delayed. She became confidential about her work, comparing it to that of a journalist, which, she suggested, was more interesting, more important, and opened the way more easily to more spacious things. Mr. Mackintosh went at last, pleased with himself in the anticipation that his paper would have a scoop next morning (for no other reporters had yet appeared), and with no doubt of the simple veracity of the girl who had been so flattering, so affable, and so frank.

"And perhaps now," Eustace said, as the sound of the motor-bike died on the coastal road, "you'll tell me what you're really meaning to do."

"What I said, of course. I thought you'd see what a good idea it is. It's no use thinking of flying back tomorrow if we're to have reporters round us as thick as flies. I hate holding things up, with Mr. Catsgill placed as he is, but it's no good trying to save time if we only get caught out in consequence.

"If any reporters come smelling round tomorrow morning they'll just learn that we've gone on the road. There's no mystery about that. They'll find it all in the *Glasgow Standard.* And if they try following us, they'll find that's really what we *have* done. When we're sure we're not being followed, we'll head south."

"What about all the luggage?"

"We shall have to leave it here, and say we'll call for it on the way back. It's a curse to have to do that, but it'll all help to prevent anyone doubting that everything's going to be just as we say."

"You seem to have thought it out thoroughly! I suppose it's the best course, now that the police have let everyone know where we came. I can't help having some doubt about the wisdom of that."

But Billie was in good spirits and indisposed to be critical, even of Inspector Cauldron. She said she thought it was rather subtle. If Mr. Mildew read it—and it was certain to come to his notice if he were giving any thought to them at all—he might think the press had got it either from themselves or the police (he'd have to guess that), but he'd conclude that there was no thought of hiding from him. What Inspector Cauldron wanted him to think was that they hadn't given him away, and that they neither needed protection nor were of any further interest to Scotland Yard—and then, they having gone such a distance away, he wasn't likely to trouble further about them. "And as to making it hard for us to get back," she concluded, "that's about the last thing the police expect or want us to do. They reckon they can give Mr. Catsgill all the protection he needs without any help from us."

"Well, we must hope they're right.... You'd better tell the land-lady about our new plans. Considering what you said when we came—"

But Billie said she could easily manage that.

CHAPTER III.

Which Ends in a Scotch Mist

A YOUNG lady who has supported herself for nearly four years by undertaking research work for irregular clients at the British Museum has learned to subsist upon a moderate and somewhat precarious income. She will have realized the value of money and the annoyances (far greater than any benefits it can give) which its absence may cause. Unless she be incurably improvident, it is unlikely, at the end of such a period, that she will be careless in its expenditure, even should the possibility become hers.

Billie had no disposition to dissipate the ninety-one pound notes which lay, neatly banded together and taking surprisingly little space, in her own suitcase, or the larger sum which was in her brother's possession; but there are occasions when money must not be grudgingly used.

The face of the landlady of the Prince's Head became grim with anticipation of battle as Billie told her that they proposed to leave after an early breakfast next morning; but before she could object that the room had been taken at a weekly rental (an error for which Eustace bore the sole responsibility), it cleared with the following announcement that they would return—probably within a fortnight—and would like to come to terms to leave their luggage and retain the rooms in the meantime.

This being finally agreed at a figure which was two-thirds of her first proposal and one-third more than she had expected to get, Mrs. Cameron became loquacious in advice as to the route her guests should take and the natural beauties they must not omit to see. As Billie listened, with this advice supplementing that which she had heard from Alexander Mackintosh at an earlier hour, the projected tour assumed an objective reality in her own mind which made it easier to respond in convincing tones.

When they left early next morning, their minds divided between consciousness of the weights they carried and regrets for many things unavoidably left behind, the tale of their projected wanderings had gained a detailed particularity, so that the more searching the enquiries that might be made concerning it, the more convincing it would become. "And all the trouble," Billie concluded, "more likely than not for just nothing at all! I'd say it's ten to one that Mr. Mildew hasn't given us a thought since he read that we were flying to Oban, even if he hadn't lost interest in us before that. He must have plenty else on his mind just now."

"I suppose he has," Eustace agreed; "though he probably feels that he's been too much for Scotland Yard, which isn't as far from the truth as we'd like it to be. He'd probably be quite content to leave us alone here, taking it as good enough evidence that we should be no further nuisance to him. I expect he's just as much inclined as the police to lie low for a time.

"But it seems to me that the position's less simple than that. There's the question of whether Catsgill recovers, and what he'll say if he does. And, apart from that, if Mildew thinks I haven't given him away, he'll be expecting me to look to him for a job when we get back to London."

"He won't do that. Whether he thinks we gave him away or not, he won't trust us again. You can tell that from what happened to Mr. Catsgill, and what I'm sure he meant to happen to us."

"I dare say you're right; and, if so, it only means that any security we have now would only continue till we should return to London. But it only strengthens what I was trying to say, that, even if he's taking no interest in us here, he'd be taking an unpleasant amount the moment he heard that we were on our way back. We can't be too careful how we act now, if we're to hope to do any good, apart from taking care of ourselves."

"There's one good point about being up here. As long as we want to make ourselves conspicuous, it'll be easy to leave a trail that no one could miss."

"Yes. We ought soon to be able to make sure whether we're being followed or not; though we know so few of the gang that I don't see how we could be sure."

"Oh, but we should make a fair guess. And I was just thinking what a good thing it will be when we get back to London that most of them can't have seen either of us. We might meet them anywhere without their having the least suspicion."

"They don't even know each other, most of them. They don't even know Mildew. That isn't his way."

Eustace saw that it was the fact that they *did* know Mildew that placed them in such particular peril. Even long-trusted members of the gang in responsible positions had no knowledge of who might be its directing head. Mildew would need to have a much greater confidence both in their loyalty and discretion than he would have reason to feel, to tolerate that they should know or suspect so much as they had had reason to do. Eustace thought, as Mr. Catsgill had done before, that there could be no safety for anyone with such confidential knowledge unless Mildew were within the strong walls of an English jail. But why say it? He saw that Billie was in the mood to confront anything in a sanguine spirit. What harm was there in that?

He knew that she would be alert, shrewd, resourceful if a moment of danger should come upon them. She did not ignore facts because she took them with a gay optimism. And the thought that they would never be certain of safety while Mildew remained at large and at the head of his ruthless gang gave an appearance of prudence, of self-defence, to the hazard of this projected return to the scene of his unlawful activities. Beyond that, Eustace was resolved that she should not again be involved in any separate peril. They would keep together in future. It would be hard to persuade him to depart from that resolution. But, as he thought this, Billie said: "I've been thinking, when we do decide to head south, that it'll be best to travel different ways, and meet in London somewhere that we both know."

Here was subject for debate to occupy them for the next hour as they toiled an ascending road, but in the end Billie won conditional assent to a proposal the logic of which was not easy to overset. If they observed no sign that they were followed, and if she would promise to do nothing of a hazardous nature till they should be reunited, it might really be the more prudent course.

They went northward for the next two days, covering less than thirty miles, for the roads were often steep, the days were warm, there was no temptation to exert themselves beyond inclination with the knowledge that every step took them further away from their distant goal, and, though they had an abundance of youthful vigour, they were no more accustomed to sustained pedestrianism than are most of the generation to which they belonged.

During those two days they had no reason to think that they were objects of interest to any except the aboriginal inhabitants of the picturesque but desolate regions to which they came, though they used their own names and even aimed, by conversing freely with those they met, to leave a trail that would be easy to follow.

On the third morning they turned eastwards, facing a bright sun, and a bitter wind which had risen during the night. At midday the wind fell, but the sky clouded greyly. They were on a black, stony road with rock rising on their left hand and a wide, shallow mountain tarn stretching on their right to the foot of a bare hill. There was no movement of life but the swaying reeds of the lake, and a pair of unknown birds that rose at their approach and flew low over the water with wailing cries that seemed born of the desolation in which they lived.

They had taken the precaution of providing themselves with sandwiches, and sat down on convenient stones for a wayside meal. While they halted there the rain came, or perhaps it would be more accurately described as a thick mist. The mountain on the further side of the lake became indistinct, and then faded from view.

Billie rose, shaking crumbs from a damp lap. She stooped to fasten an extra button of her raincoat. "Not," she said, "that there's much use in that. It seems to me it's the sort of rain that can come up just as well as down."

"Anyway, we'd better be getting on," Eustace agreed as he rose also. "I reckon we've got another five miles to go before we come to anything worth putting on the map, and if this mist gets any worse...."

"It's doing that all the time. Now, if someone would just come along and offer us a lift—"

"Speak of the devil," Eustace replied, for with Billie's words there had come the sound of a slowly approaching car.

"Shall we flag it to stop?"

"They wouldn't see us until they're within a few feet. We shall be able to walk alongside at the rate that they're coming now." This statement went somewhat beyond literal fact, but it was true that the mist was becoming denser and that the car was travelling slowly, as was prudent on such a road. When it reached them, there was no need to ask for that which was offered to them as it came abreast.

CHAPTER IV.

A Good Offer Is Ill Received

IT was a small Standard saloon car, new and well kept, with a liveried chauffeur driving, and a red-faced man of jovial aspect on the rear seat, who threw open an inviting door as it drew level, with a friendly "Going my way?" which assumed rather than asked that they would accept the proffered lift. "John, take the lady in front," were his next words. With scarcely time for thought or thanks, they were in the car, and it was moving again.

Billie looked at the chauffeur, who took no notice of her. His attention was on the road, as it had reason to be. They rose, twisting sharply, and then came to an abrupt descent. The road curved and narrowed. The mist closed upon them. Looking at the man's expressionless profile, she thought: "He is not one whom I should like to meet on a dark night." But, she reflected more sensibly, chauffeurs are not engaged for their looks, but for their ability to control a car. The man drove coolly and well.

Having no conversation to engage her thoughts, Billie listened to that which went on behind. Eustace was saying: "It was lucky for us you came just when you did." To which the owner of the car replied in his jolly voice: "Well, I couldn't say it was luck exactly. I'd come a good many miles to find you, Mr. Limbrook. I'd say the luck was mine not to have missed you in this diabolical fog."

There was a tone of natural surprise in Eustace's voice as he replied: "I didn't suppose that you knew us when you invited us to get in. I can't remember—"

"Remember me? I should say not! I don't suppose you ever saw me before. But everyone knows you and Miss Wingrove now. I suppose you haven't seen this?"

He pulled out from his pocket a copy of the *Glasgow Standard*, with a reproduction of one of the photographs which the reporter of that paper had taken three days before. It was—of Billie especially—good enough to explain the identification. But it did not explain why this jovial gentleman should have pursued them. So Eustace said.

"I came after you, Mr. Limbrook, because you're the man we want. I represent the Glasgow Construction Company—Bolton's my name—and we've got a job in Vancouver that's waiting for you. The salary'll be fifteen hundred with a five years' guarantee. You can't want fairer than that. The man we sent out has just died after an operation in Montréal. He never got there at all, and everything's held up till we can get someone to take his place. I want you to come back with me to Glasgow now and sail on the next boat."

Billie listened without turning her head. The offer might be genuine. She knew that Eustace's credentials were good. The testimonials of his South American appointment had gained him the position with the Rushton-Thornville Company which he had only lost through the failure of that firm, which had been no discredit to him. It was of the precarious nature of his profession that he might be twelve months without occupation, or be offered a responsible position at any moment in Cochin-China or the Australian desert. But why did his jesting words "Speak of the devil" come back to her and seem so appropriate now?

She heard Eustace say: "It sounds an attractive offer, and I'm much obliged to you for taking the trouble to get in touch with me. But I should have one or two matters to clear up before it would be possible for me to sail.... And I'm not alone, as you see. Suppose I call on you in Glasgow on Thursday morning? I think I could manage that."

Mr. Bolton's manner changed. "Huffy" was the adjective Billie mentally used for its description. "I'm afraid," he said, "I haven't made myself clear. Time is the one thing we can't spare. We're willing to be liberal about terms, but we want you to go out on the next boat. Our contract's subject to a heavy penalty clause, and we're a month behind now."

"I appreciate that. If I accept the offer—and it sounds like one I shouldn't be likely to turn down—you can rely upon me to travel without a moment's avoidable delay. But there are one or two preparations, one or two things I should be obliged to deal with before leaving. You'd expect that. And the way I propose may actually save time in the end."

But Mr. Bolton did not give way: "I'm afraid I must still ask you to put other matters aside, unless you wish to tell me that I must look in some other direction for the help we require. You'll agree that there won't be much difficulty about getting such a position filled. Come, Mr. Limbrook, we know you are on a holiday now. Just wandering about. It can't be too much to ask you to let me drive you to Glasgow. We don't want to be inconsiderate to you, but you must consider us also.

"We shall be there before evening—unless this infernal fog stops us altogether!—and we'll find a hotel for Miss Wingrove and yourself for the night. The expense is on us for that. And in the morning we'll fix the whole matter up."

"I've got all my luggage at an inn at Glairgowrie. I thought it might be the quickest way to go back there first and pick it up."

Even to Billie, listening in intent silence, and about equally anxious to judge whether it were a genuine offer and whether Eustace were prepared to accept it, even at the cost of abandoning the enterprise on which they had resolved, this excuse sounded weak.

"I believe Eustace is stalling," she thought, "and I wish I knew why he's doing that. Perhaps he doesn't trust Mr. Bolton (no more do I). But it *may* be a genuine offer. There's no sensible reason for doubting that. And even if Mr. Mildew's pulled the strings, it wouldn't prove that it isn't. He has lots of influence. We've seen that already. I suppose most business men have, if they are as wealthy as he. It might be his way of getting Eustace to go abroad before the police would have any chance of getting at him again."

It was a reflection which left her in doubt of what would be the best for Eustace, or even what she would wish him to do. Such an offer is not lightly to be refused in favour of pushing one's way unasked into other people's troubles.

But, if he should go, would she be willing to give up the investigation on which she had set her heart? Not at all. She was not even *quite* sure that she might not feel a sense of satisfaction in having it entirely in her own hands. Her mind went forward to an imaginary moment of triumph when she would say to Inspector Cauldron: "Here's the proof which all you clever detectives have given up (well, for the time, at least) trying to find!" That would be pleasant enough, though she owned in a candid mind that she and they would not be starting from scratch, for she had the address which Mr. Catsgill had given her, which was unknown to them. Actually, that was all on which she was building these easy dreams. She had done nothing whatever. And the address might be an utter dud! Also, it suddenly occurred to her, the police might have got it before now, though they had not when she left London. Mr. Catsgill had been lying unconscious in hospital, with a police officer (it was simple to guess) not far from his bed-head. Suppose, on recovering his wits, that the first murmured words had been the address which he had given to her? Suppose that she should contrive to get back to London by a circuitous route and advance to the investigation of 4, Adam Street, with precautions vaguely imagined, only to meet Inspector Cauldron leading handcuffed prisoners from the door?

Well, anyhow, that would mean that justice was being done, and she would be able to resume her work at the Museum with freedom from the shadow of peril which, however resiliently she had reacted to it, had lain upon her both day and night since the evening when she had outwitted (but had she?) the bullying Wellard at the Reader Grill.

All this was on the assumption that Eustace might be sailing to Vancouver on Thursday, leaving her to a single battle of wits with the Mildew Gang. And that, her reason told her, was the one thing that it was certain he would not do. It might be, indeed, that he saw no reason to doubt the good faith of the offer he had received, and that, if he were stalling now, it was only because he would commit himself to nothing before he had her promise to leave danger alone.

That was an unpleasant thought, because, though she could not reconcile herself to giving up the struggle into which she had been so strangely drawn, neither could she contemplate with a quiet mind Eustace's prospects being spoiled by her stubborn whim.

But was the danger really so great? Remembering what had happened to Mr. Catsgill, she could not doubt its reality. And this thought brought up a more sinister possibility. She had been considering the preferable explanations that the offer was the straightforward business proposition which it purported to be, or else that it had been instigated by Mr. Mildew to get Eustace out of the way. There remained the more threatening possibility that it might have no substance at all.

Suppose that they were being taken for a ride in the American sense of that innocent phrase? She did not seriously suppose that they would be shot in the next ten minutes and their bodies thrown from the car. She credited Mildew with a subtler, more inventive mind, though she saw, with a heartbeat's pause, that the mist would be friendly to such a crime.

But if they were being taken to some sinister destination, prompt action was imperative for the frustration of such a danger. And in its own way the mist was friendly to Eustace and her. The car was not moving now at more than eight or ten miles an hour. To open the door and jump quickly out would not have been an impossible or very dangerous enterprise, if only there were any possibility of establishing a prior understanding with Eustace, so that they would act together. But such an attempt, singly made, would bring crisis in a form difficult to forecast, about which the best which could be certainly thought was that, if it must come, it might be better to have it at their own time than that of their captors, if such they were. And yet—did she wish that time to be in the mist, in this lonely place?

The doubt naturally led her on to consider where they were going and how soon they might come to town or village where such a demonstration might be more safely made, or where she might advance some pretext of hunger or illness to secure a stoppage which would, at least, provide opportunity for the private words with Eustace which the position required. And if they were once out of the car, it would not be easy to get them back, except at their own choice.

They had studied the map carefully together that morning, and she had looked at it again as they had rested beside the way. They were now going almost due east. She was sure of that. She would have thought that the best way of reaching Glasgow would have been to turn the car round immediately that it had caught them up. She might be wrong about that. Possibly it would be better to go on and turn south by some road ahead. She had not looked at the map with Glasgow in mind, and routes are treacherous to guess. But one thing she *knew*. The road forked at a point which they must now be near to reach.

If the car should take the right-hand way, it would prove nothing; but if it should take the left, it would be certain that Glasgow was not their goal.

What should she do then? In preference to attempting to jump out alone, might she not upset the car? A sudden clutch at the wheel might do that, and a plea of accidental folly could not be certainly disproved.

The car, after a short spurt of speed—for the mist was becoming patchy—was moving slowly again. There would be little risk now. There was a shallow ditch on the near side. If the near wheels should descend into that, the car would certainly be stopped. The side of the ditch was too deep and abrupt for the wheels to remount it. So, rightly or wrongly, she thought. But she also thought that the car might fall over upon its side. Yet, at the pace they were going, she saw little danger in that. But she considered that Eustace and she would be underneath. The chauffeur would, be upon her, and Eustace would be sustaining Mr. Bolton's much more considerable weight. These were not positions to choose, even had their companions been more congenial than they were.... She would wait, at least, till they should come to the forking roads. If the car should take the right-hand way, as was reasonable to expect, she knew that they would come to a village not more than half a mile ahead.

CHAPTER V.

A Use for a Good Ditch

EUSTACE had consented now. Billie had missed a few words as she had considered overturning the car and matters cognate thereto; but it was clear from what was being said that he had given way to Mr. Bolton's logic or importunity, and had agreed to be driven straight to Glasgow. The proposal now was that they should stop at the nearest railway station and that Billie should return to Glairgowrie alone, where he could telephone her to send or bring his luggage to the boat, if he should accept the appointment.

She saw that, if this should be agreed, it would be far better than overturning the car. At the railway station they would naturally both get out. That could scarcely be prevented when they had pulled up. And if they should change their minds, they could both get into the train, and that—for the moment—would be the end of *that*.

But Mr. Bolton, though in the mollified tone of one who felt he was getting his own way, was opposing this suggestion also. He said that it would be best for them to keep together till they got to Glasgow, and Miss Wingrove could travel from there to Glairgowrie more conveniently in the morning. Finding Eustace slow to agree, he became argumentative to a point which weakened his own case. Billie knew enough of the geography of the country to be sure that to travel to Glairgowrie via Glasgow from where they were was an absurdity to suggest. She was sure also that they were within a few miles of an appropriate station for her to use. And that station lay to the south, as Glasgow certainly did. Mr. Bolton could easily put her down there, if he would. And why should he object?

But object he did. He was arguing now that, however willing his firm might be to make the appointment, they might resent an *assumption* that it would be made, and she saw that that was absurd,

27

even apart from the fact that it was inconsistent with how he had talked before.

There was no assumption implied in her returning to the inn where their luggage was. Rather the other way. The conclusion that he had a different reason for wishing to keep her in the car became irresistible, and with it the cold conviction that that reason must be hostile to her. With the thought she was aware of the forking roads and of a signpost at their junction. She could not read what it said: the mist at this point was too dense for that. But she saw that the chauffeur, without asking for instructions, without hesitation, took the left-hand way. At the same moment there came the sound of another car that was coming toward them at a more rapid pace than their own, and hooting its dread of the blinding road.

The ditch was still there, at her left hand. Perhaps rather deeper than before. It might be her best—perhaps her last—chance. Any moment they might break into, clearer air and the pace quicken.

She turned her head toward the occupants of the rear seat. "From what I can overhear," she said lightly, "you seem to be making plans for me without asking my opinion concerning them."

She saw that the chauffeur had his eyes on the road. He took no notice of her. His own horn was now sounding insurgent warning to the approaching car.

"My dear young lady," Mr. Bolton began, "what I propose is— " It was a sentence he was not destined to finish.

As he spoke she had turned further, as though to give him her attention, and, as she did so, as though to steady herself, her right hand caught the steering-wheel, with a gesture which appeared casual, but she pulled on it with all the strength that the position allowed.

For half a second it came round with scarcely any resistance. Then she felt it was in a reversing grip stronger than she could control. But the harm was done. The front near wheel had slipped over the edge. Almost simultaneously the rear one followed. The car lurched forward a few yards, throwing its occupants roughly about, and then, with a sound of buckling metal and bending wood, pitched over upon its side.

Billie, less conscious of several bruises than she would be at a later hour, was aware of the chauffeur's body pressing upon her own, and then of his struggles to reach a door which was now over their heads. His words, as he did this, were foul and his actions rough. He may not have intended to kick her or to use her legs as a foundation on which to ground his efforts to force open a wedged door, but that is what he did, and his intentions, good or bad, made no difference to her.

She squirmed backward, but found that there could be no retreat into the rear of the car, for the portly body of Mr. Bolton had been thrown forward, and that of Eustace was underneath. Mr. Bolton was breathing heavily, but gave no other sign of conscious life. She could not be sure that Eustace was breathing at all. At that moment, had it been in her power to do so, she would have righted the car and let it take her to whatever precarious fate might have been in that hard-breathing gentleman's mind, but the game of life cannot be played in that way. It has a stage on which rehearsals are not allowed.

The chauffeur strove savagely, letting his feet find leverage where they would, but his position was unfavourable. Actually, that made no difference. The door was jammed beyond moving by any exertion of human muscles. Neither could the glass be let down.

Someone was kneeling on the car now, trying to open the door, with no more success. After a hard pull these efforts were transferred to the rear door, with better results. It rose and was swung back, letting in air and light.

The face of a young woman, a cigarette still hanging from her lips, looked down upon them. "Anyone hurt?" she asked unemotionally. "Can you manage if I give you a hand?"

The chauffeur was already clambering over the back of his seat. His regard for his employer's body appeared to be no more than for Billie's legs. But the treatment may have been that which the occasion required, for, as the man wriggled upward, ignoring the proffered hand, Mr. Bolton's voice became articulate in angry protest.

"Keep your clumsy feet off me, you damned fool," he exclaimed as, breathing more loudly than before, he strove to raise himself to the light above.

But getting him out proved to be a slow and formidable operation. He ignored no proffered hand. The chauffeur hauled, and the young lady gave vigorous help in a careless manner. Slowly the obese body was drawn aloft.

Relieved of Bolton's weight, Eustace came to life in a quieter way. "You're not hurt?" he whispered.

"No. Only kicked to pieces. And you?"

"Oh, I'm all right. You did splendidly. Listen quickly. Separate at the first chance, and meet at the Charles Hotel, Eccleston Square. You can remember that, Eccleston Square—Charles Hotel, behind Victoria Station."

"You think they're crooks?"

"I know they are. The chauffeur's got a gun in his hip pocket."

"I'm not going to leave you with them."

"Don't spoil everything now. I'm not going to stay with them. But I'm not going till you've gone, so the sooner you find an excuse to quit, the better it will—"

The increase of light above demonstrated that the body of Mr. Bolton had cleared the door. Eustace ceased the whispered conversation abruptly. "You next," he said.

"No. I can manage better when you're out of the way."

"Nonsense. Go ahead."

"But I shall want you to help me out."

Eustace saw reason in that. She might reasonably prefer his assistance to that of the gentleman who had already emerged. He wasted no further time on the point of etiquette, but clambered out, and reached a hand to Billie, who was up as nimbly, though not without consciousness of the bruises she had endured.

The four dishevelled occupants of the car looked at one another, and speech was slow to come. The other three were, from different angles, waiting to observe Mr. Bolton's reaction to the disconcerting event, and that gentleman had been too badly shaken for his wits to function with normal celerity. When they did, he became conscious of a dilemma with which it would not have been easy to determine how best to deal, even had he not been obsessed by fear of one whose instructions he had been carrying out, and who was not gentle to those who failed.

The fifth member of the party considered the aspects of those whom she had been active to rescue, and decided that they were not really chummy. She broke the silence with, "I suppose you'll say this was my fault for honking to you to get out of the way."

This surprisingly generous misinterpretation of the event had the effect of drawing all eyes upon the speaker, a slenderly built, even lean young woman of an obviously sporting type, who appeared to be coolly amused at the catastrophe which she so readily attributed to her own mishandling of the large primrose-yellow touring car which now occupied more than half the breadth of the narrow road, and of which she appeared to have been the only occupant.

Billie felt it to be a disconcerting remark. Obviously, she could not let this entirely innocent young lady accept responsibility for her own action, but she was unsure how far it was known, or its deliberation guessed, by those before whom she must speak, and was discreet enough to delay a confession which might be made at a better time.

The chauffeur opened his mouth, but gave utterance to no more than an inarticulate exclamation. It told her that he, at least, realized what had occurred, would. But his eyes went to his employer, and he also doubted whether it were the moment for candid speech.

Mr. Bolton was left to reply. He said: "That is a matter with which the insurance companies will have to deal."

"I'm not sure how that would be. The cars didn't collide. But I expect they'd agree that it was my fault. I've been in so much trouble before. In fact, if you don't mind, I'd rather pay for any damage there is and not trouble them about it at all."

Saying this, the young lady produced a card. Mr. Bolton learned that he had met the world-famous racing motorist, the Hon. Gloria Brell, of Brell Castle, Argyll. He said, with some recovery of the jovial manner which was a cultivated veneer, covering a particularly cowardly, cunning, and brutal character: "It's as you like about that. But I shouldn't say there's much damage done." He turned to the chauffeur, who was already clambering round the overturned car, to ask: "How about getting it going again? Can you manage that?"

The man was not hopeful. He thought the engine was all right, and they might get the car jacked up (if they had a jack) so that it could be got back on to the road, but the back axle was buckled, and how serious the damage might be it was impossible to say while the car lay as it did.

"That's awkward," Billie said innocently. "We were on our way to Glasgow, and wanted to be there this evening."

Miss Brell stared at that. "Glasgow?" she exclaimed. "I rather thought I was on the way there myself. One of us must have been going the wrong way."

"You mean this isn't the road to Glasgow?"

"Well, it would be rather better for Aberdeen."

"I'm afraid," Mr. Bolton said, "we must have missed our way in the fog."

"Yes," Miss Brell replied dryly, "you certainly must." She did not pursue the subject further. She said: "There's a good garage about a mile along the road you just passed. They'll do anything necessary to the car, and charge it to me. But you don't look like getting anywhere in it tonight. I'll drive you to Glasgow, if that will be any help. There's lots of room in mine."

"It's very kind of you," Billie said, "especially as we're not sure it was your fault at all. Mr. Limbrook and I will be glad to come…. Eustace, what about getting our things out of the car?"

Billie had observed that, since he had learned that the car could not be started again, Mr. Bolton had had the look of a troubled man. She felt sure that his plans had gone wrong beyond immediate re-construction, and it would not have required much inducement for her to make frank admission of how and why she had wrecked the car. "We can all get to Glasgow now, Mr. Bolton," she went on, "rather more quickly than we should have been likely to do the way we were going; so perhaps it wasn't a bad thing that it happened the way it did." She gave him her sweetest smile as she said this, but his response was what she had half expected and entirely hoped it to be. He had no desire to take any road that led in the direction of Glas-gow. In fact, he had never had such an intention. Now he made ex-cuse that he must stand by the car until the men from the garage should arrive to take charge of it. He would send the chauffeur to fetch them.

Miss Brell accepted this solution easily, though she made a fur-ther offer. "That's for you to say. But if you like to come on and leave your man here, I'll drive you round to the garage, and we'll give them the necessary instructions."

Mr. Bolton thanked her, but said that he had his luggage to think of. There were things of value he must not risk. He would probably decide to hire another car. He might not be coming to Glasgow immediately now. The accident had altered his plans.

Miss Brell repeated indifferently: "Well, that's for you to say." Eustace asked: "I suppose I'd better call at the office of the Glasgow Construction Company in the morning? Or shall I leave it till you will have got back?"

The veneer of gentility which Mr. Bolton wore was insufficient to receive this question complacently. "You'll be wasting your time if you do," he replied, with a vicious look in his eyes. "Not after what's happened here."

"Perhaps it's just as well. It's the first time I've heard of the firm. The offices mightn't have been easy to find."

Mr. Bolton, having recovered his self-control, gave no sign of perceiving the implications of this retort. Eustace climbed down into the overturned car and rescued the burdens which those who take pedestrian tours are obliged to bear.

The mist was thinning now, as though having accomplished the purpose for which it came. There was weak sunlight and a movement of chilly wind.

Eustace and Billie mounted to the front seat of the primrose tourer, which was spacious enough for three people to sit abreast.

Mr. Bolton, as they passed from sight, turned to his assistant to say: "You'd better get to that garage in double-quick time. Tell them to send a car for me to use, and get on yourself to the nearest call-box and ring up Mitchell and tell him what's happened. Say I'll be phoning him myself in an hour's time. That'll give him time to simmer down and get his own instructions from higher up."

The man took these instructions sullenly. He understood that he was to take the first brunt of the anger that the report would rouse. But it was not primarily his responsibility. He said no more than, "For all the softies they were, they've made proper fools of us." But the tone implied that the plural pronoun was of diplomatic rather than literal use.

CHAPTER VI.

Stirling Will Do

THE HON. Gloria Brell was one by whom no one should sit in a fast car unless having good nerves and a sound heart, or the obtuseness which is too foolish to fear. She took the sharp curves of the mountain road at a pace which may have been correctly judged as the highest to half a second which was consistent with safety. Indeed, so it must have been, for no accident resulted; but it was one which, for most drivers, would have ensured them a broken neck. She did this with one hand seeming to rest only loosely upon the wheel, while she passed her cigarette-case to her companions, and expressed her candid view of those they had left behind.

"I didn't think they were friends of yours. They both looked lousy to me. And I saw that chauffeur glare at you when you were getting in here as though he'd have brained you with a spanner if he'd had you by himself in a quiet place."

The last part of this remark was addressed to Billie, who replied to it with equal candour: "I've no doubt he would. In fact, I think that's very much what the programme was before I gave him any cause to feel that way. But he wasn't likely to be in a good temper after what I'd done, and that leads up to what I've been wanting to tell you. You mustn't pay for repairing the car. It was no fault of yours. It ran into the ditch on purpose. The man wasn't likely to feel pleased."

Miss Brell looked a natural surprise. "I didn't know you were driving. Why on earth did you do that?"

"I wasn't driving. I just put a hand on the wheel."

"But why did you? You're not one to do a fool trick like that."

"It was really because I heard you coming along."

"You don't mind making it a bit clearer?"

"I thought it might be quite a good idea to change cars."

"Serious as that, was it?"

"So I thought. For one thing, we seemed to be going to Glasgow by a very unusual road."

"So you certainly were. But it was a neat piece of work. If they were intending to murder you in a quiet spot, you must have shaken up their plans quite a lot."

Miss Brell showed no lack of interest in the event, but her attitude to the idea of being abducted with murderous aims was as casual as had been confined in the wrecked car. Billie wondered whether the precarious nature of the life of a racing driver might account for this emotionless reaction. If you are exposed to possibilities of sudden death or unimaginable mutilations every day of the week, it can scarcely be possible to maintain excitement at a pitch which those who live less hazardous lives might consider appropriate to such risks. Miss Brell went on: "Would it be impertinent to ask how you came to be in the fat gentleman's car?"

"Oh, they'd caught us up on the road, and offered to give us a lift. It seemed a good idea, with the fog as thick as it was."

"And to take you to Glasgow, although you must have been going the opposite way?"

"We weren't doing that. We were resting at the side of the road. And we weren't going to Glasgow either. That idea only developed after we got in the car."

Eustace had listened silently to these confusing verbal exchanges. He saw that Billie's literal answers, accurate though they were, were not of a clearly informative character. But the continuation of conversation on these lines must end in complete disclosure explicit lies, or a blunt refusal to give intelligible explanation of what had been already said. He was himself half disposed to a full confidence, and he had learned that Billie could be discreet, and would be likely to be deliberate in what she did. For the moment she should go her own way, without attempt of interference from him.

Miss Brell's next question, in any event, was one to which they could not object to reply: "I suppose you do really want to go to Glasgow?"

"Not particularly," Billie replied. "Certainly not to take you out of your own way. But we understood you were going there."

"I'm on my way to Brooklands. It doesn't matter to me which road I take. I'm not particular as to a few miles more or less. If you'll tell me what you're really wanting to do—"

They were passing along the narrow winding street of a picturesque Scottish village as they came to this point of the conversation, and Gloria Brell had slowed down to the moderate pace which its negotiation imperatively required, for there was a pedlar's barrow standing unattended in the middle of a roadway on which children played. Further on was a char-a-banc loaded with holiday makers, drawn up at the door of the village inn.

It was the sight of this vehicle which inspired Billie's surprising reply: "What I really want to do is to get on to that char-a-banc, if they've got a seat to spare."

Eustace said: "That wouldn't be such a bad idea."

Miss Brell said: "You don't mind where it's going? Well, you know your own business best!"

Her foot pressed the brake, and she stopped smoothly beside the standing vehicle, with no more than inches of clearance in the width of the narrow street. She called to the conductor, who was loitering at the inn door: "Have you two seats to spare?"

"One seat," Billie corrected quickly.

"I hoped," Eustace explained, "you wouldn't mind taking me a little further."

Miss Brell said no more than "Oh!" and then, "No, not at all. It's just as you like."

The conductor said they could find room for one. Billie collected her belongings. "You won't do anything till I get there? You'll promise that?" she asked as she rose.

Eustace answered reasonably: "How could I? I don't even know the address. If you mentioned it, I've forgotten—"

"I don't want you not to have that. Suppose something happened that I couldn't— It *was* M. Beal. No 'E' at the end. And the address was 4, Adam Street. But you'll wait for me. Yes, I remember, Charles Hotel. Eccleston Square…. Goodbye, Miss Brell. I shall have to leave Eustace to thank you properly for all you've done for us."

Billie did not descend to the street. There would not have been space to open the car door. She mounted from one vehicle to the other. "Stirling?" she replied to the conductor, who had climbed up to receive her. "Yes. That will do as well as anywhere else." She waved a hand to Eustace as the car moved out of sight down the crooked street.

Miss Brell was saying: "And now perhaps you won't mind telling me what all this means?"

CHAPTER VII.

By Devious Ways

BILLIE WINGROVE did not see the primrose car pass out of sight without becoming conscious of a feeling of loneliness which was a near cousin to fear. The experience through which she had passed would have been a nervous ordeal for anyone more accustomed than herself to episodes of physical danger, and the knowledge which it had brought that Eustace and she were still objects of the ruthless pursuit of the Mildew Gang was a test of courage which many would have failed to sustain.

But she faced this feeling boldly, and found, as may often be, that reason diminished fear. The game had still to be won, but she saw that when her hand pulled on the steering-wheel she had trumped the immediate trick. She saw also that the police had been wrong when they had concluded that Mr. Mildew would lose interest in Eustace and herself if he were made aware that they had left London. And if there were to be no safety for them, even in distant places, while Mildew remained in control of his lawless gang, then prudence might approve their return to renew the fight. That being so, the first essential was to get back to London unfollowed, which should not be difficult now. On the whole, she told herself resolutely, she must call it a good day....

It was four days later that she arrived at the Charles Hotel, to find that Eustace was already there.

"How did I get here?" she echoed his question. "Oh, from somewhere on the South Coast. I can't remember before that! I trained from there to Horsham, took a side line to East Grinstead, then a Green Line coach to Croydon, and from there on a bus into Belgrave Road. If they can spot people entering London by such ways as that they must have more spies about than even the dope trade, or Mildew's fortune, could pay. If you took as many precautions as I did, we shan't have made a bad start."

"I don't think I've done badly. I thought it best to tell the whole tale. She isn't one to talk, and it panned out well. She saw it wouldn't do for her to drive me into London. If they were making the most elementary efforts to trace us, they would be sure to be on the watch for her car, seeing that she gave her name to Bolton when she drove us away; and she couldn't delay her own plans. She was bound to come straight on for Brooklands. But she helped me, all the same, in a better way than I could have managed alone. When we were in Durham she telephoned to a friend in Yorkshire to meet her at a lonely spot on the moors, and she—a Mrs. Bentley, who was a real sport—drove me right across the country into Cheshire, and put me down at a little station where there certainly wasn't anyone about of the wrong sort. I travelled from there into Wales, and came here much as you seem to have done, partly by coaches and partly by trains, and ending up on a trolley-bus from Uxbridge to Shepherd's Bush. I got here last night, after dark, and registered in a false name."

"I suppose I'd better do the same."

"Yes. And act as though we are only casual acquaintances, who just exchange a few words as we happen to meet in the lounge here."

Billie saw the wisdom of this. She went back to the hotel office, which she had walked past on first entering, asked for a room in the name of Miss Mary Smithson, and forestalled any possible challenge on the score of her meagre luggage by saying: "I don't suppose I shall be here more than one night, so I may as well pay you now."

The reception clerk pushed the book over for her to sign with a routine courtesy but little interest, for the Charles Hotel depends for most of its custom upon those who come and go through the great clearinghouse of Victoria Station, and an actual majority of them stay for no more than a single night. From the managerial standpoint they are of only two qualities—those who do, and those who do not, haggle about their bills; and Billie proved to be one of the better sort.

Later in the evening she met Eustace in the smoking-room, which was deserted except by an American gentleman, who dozed between frequent drinks. Even so, Eustace was too cautious for speech. He passed over a slip of paper on which he had written: "Imprudent to stay here. Hotels may be looked over. Have been out and taken a room at 19, Fordyce Street. Another fourth-floor room vacant there. You should secure it tomorrow." There was a post-script: "Look at M. Beal in the Telephone Directory in the writing-room."

Billie nodded response at a moment when there was certainty that she could not be observed. She strolled out to the writing-room. There she read: "Beal, Maurice. Importer of Wild Animals. 4, Adam Street." There was no reticence about this announcement. It was printed in the large type for which a fee must be paid. It was plain, at least, that they had not made their hazardous return to the neighbourhood of an unscrupulous foe to find that the address Mr. Catsgill had given was no more than a mistaken memory or deserted dwelling.

CHAPTER VIII.

THE QUESTION OF WHO SHALL GO

THERE were three bed-sitting rooms and a bathroom on the fourth floor of 19, Fordyce Street. Eustace had taken one, and Billie secured the second of these. The third was let to a business young woman who was out for five days of the week from 8:45 A.M. until 6:15 at night.

The custom of the house was to serve breakfasts, but no other meal. Beyond that, there were gas stoves in the rooms, and guests could cater for themselves, if they would. After some perfunctory morning attention from an overworked maid, few things were more certain than that no one would ascend the fourth-floor stairs, besides the two new tenants, until 6:15. To the proprietress they were Mr. Springfield and Miss Mary Smithson, who had taken their rooms separately and who were strangers to one another. So long as they were discreet in going and coming separately, and confining conversation to the solitude of their own floor, it was unlikely that their acquaintance would be suspected. The next morning was given to urgent shipping, and at midday, when they could rely upon an uninterrupted conference, they met in Eustace's room to decide how they should proceed to the investigation of Mr. Beal.

"I had a look while I was out," Eustace said, "at a classified trade directory. It described him as specializing in reptiles, and generally in the fauna of South America."

"It's the continent," he continued, "where the drugs which are the basis of most dope—cocaine, heroin, and others—are produced. There may be some connection in that."

"Yes, there may…. The first thing to do is for one of us to have a look at the place and see what sort of a man Mr. Beal is."

"One of us? Why not both?"

"Because, if they've circulated any warning about us, the two of us would be far more likely to rouse suspicion than either alone."

"Yes. That's sound. And as you say that Catsgill told you he drinks, I might be able to get him to talk, if I took him round to the corner pub."

"Don't be silly, Eustace. The first time you call at a man's shop you think he'll go out with you like that? I've got a much better idea."

"Well, what is it?"

"I shall go there to buy a pet."

"What sort of a pet?"

"I've no idea. What sorts can be found among South American beasts?"

"You might ask for a parrot. But isn't there a slump in that trade owing to their having some disease they don't keep to themselves? A monkey might be better. He'd be almost sure to have some of them."

"I hate monkeys. I think the best way will be to go with an open mind. I want a pet for myself, or a wedding present for someone who's mad on beasts, but I haven't decided what. That gives an excuse for a good look round, and, of course, I shall need Mr. Beal's advice."

"I don't see why you assume you should be the one to go. I might want to buy an animal just as much as you."

"Yes, perhaps so. But Mr. Catsgill chose me for this. He knew it was a woman's work. I shall get a lot more out of Mr. Beal than you would be likely to do. That's plain sense. If it were a woman who kept the shop, it might be a bit different. But even then there'd be the disadvantage that men never see anything."

"You mean I might overlook things that you would notice?"

"Might isn't the word. Any woman sees more in a glance than she can tell in an hour, and with a man it's just the other way round. That's why women talk more than men. It's just that you can't pour out of a pint pot."

"I know I oughtn't to let you go. But we won't argue. We'll toss up."

With some difficulty, Billie, who had set her heart on being the one to invade Mr. Beal's establishment, was persuaded to agree to this method of decision, and had her reward when she called "heads" and the spun halfpenny came down displaying the bearded profile of King George V.

It was agreed, after some further argument, that they should go together as far as the Whitechapel Road, and that Eustace should then wait in the vicinity for her return.

"And if you're not soon back," he added, "I shall come along to make sure that there's nothing wrong."

"Anything wrong?" she echoed. "What could be? You don't suppose that Mr. Beal's real peculiarity is that he uses his customers to feed the beasts, do you? And if he did, there wouldn't be much use in following me into the shop to be treated the same way. It would be a saner thing to call the police.

"Besides, South American beasts aren't ferocious. Not lions and tigers and bears. Everyone knows that. They're just repulsive. Armadillos and anteaters, and—well, I'm not sure about skunks. I dare say lizards would be a better guess."

"Or pumas. And there are a few others you wouldn't care to meet alone on a dark night, though I can quite believe that Maurice Beal is the worst scene if you don't rejoin me in half an hour."

"That's nonsense. You'd spoil everything just as Beal and I would be getting chummy. Say an hour, and we'll call it a deal."

"Half an hour would be quite long enough. What do you suppose would be going to happen? Do you think he'll take you into partnership the first time you walk into the shop?"

"Well, queerer things have happened than that. Especially if I should offer to put some money into it. I expect it wants more capital. Every business does that I ever heard of. What about letting me have that £2,000 cheque? He'd have a shock looking at how it's signed!"

"I couldn't do that, because I banked it this morning. But I do wish you'd be serious. If you'll agree that I wait half an hour, and then...."

"I'll say three-quarters. Or forty minutes, if you'll agree to that without any more argument. But it's all silly. What's going to happen to me in an Adam Street shop where no one can possibly be expecting me to walk in? But if I'm not back with you inside forty minutes, you can follow me up, or, better still, give Inspector Cauldron a phone call and let him know where we both are. I should like to see Superintendent Backwash's face when he'd heard that."

"He mightn't be quite as surprised as you'd think. I'd forgotten to tell you that I'd sent him a telegram after you got on the char-a-banc."

"To tell him we were coming back to London? Eustace, you never did!"

"Not to say that. Just to give him the address of a garage where a member of the Mildew Gang, using the name of Bolton, was having a car repaired which he had employed in an unsuccessful attempt to kidnap Miss Wilhelmina Wingrove."

"Did you sign it?"

"Yes. But I put no address. I couldn't choose about that. I'd got none to put."

"Do you think there was much sense in doing that? Or was it Miss Brell's idea?"

"How did you guess that? She thought it would be sure to get the police busy, and even if they'd nothing against Bolton on which they could run him in, and he hadn't stolen the car, they'd be sure to go smelling round, and it would give him something to think of besides being nasty to us. I thought it was rather a good idea."

"You would." Billie's voice was cold, and Eustace was not too dull to perceive that she regarded his confidences to Miss Brell without enthusiasm. But next moment her lips curved to a smile. "What a flurry you must have put all those detectives into! Set all their great brains boiling with nothing, so to speak, in the pot for them to cook up. And it's no more than they deserved for sending us off to Scotland, as though we couldn't help *them*, and they knew we'd be out of mischief there. And *safe*! We were to be safe—that was the great idea. Inspector Cauldron'd find that he'd have to start thinking again!"

It was an aspect of the matter to which Eustace had not been entirely indifferent. They would have his telegram, giving no address, which they would be unlikely to ignore.

They would try to get in touch with him and Billie, and certainly fail—that had been proved by the passage of time. Indeed, they had no chance, for Miss Brell's conspicuous car had not stopped outside the telegraph office, but in a nearby street. They would make a more successful enquiry concerning Bolton and his damaged car. But unless they had means of making him speak, they were not likely to learn any luminous truth from him.

Yes, they would be perturbed, puzzled, aware that their forecasts had been incorrect, wondering what the next development would be, and utterly foiled in their endeavour to trace those whom it had become their duty to guard.

"Yes," he agreed, "I suppose it did make them dance."

On this cheerful note they set out, Billie going a few minutes first, with an understanding that she would wait at the Victoria Underground Station until he should appear, when they would book separately, but enter the same compartment of the train.

She told herself that she was not afraid—that there was, indeed, nothing to fear—that she was no more than pleasantly excited by the prospect of discovering a man so essential to the Mildew Gang that he must be protected at a great price, and even the dangerous habit of drunkenness be condoned. But the fact was that her mind had become intrigued by its own conception of grotesquely malignant creatures surrounding the sinister figure of the menagerie proprietor; and she found satisfaction in the thought that Eustace would not be distant, nor slow to come to her relief if she should be detained in the place of beasts.

CHAPTER IX.

ANACONDAS ARE NOT BOA CONSTRICTORS

THE name of Maurice Beal was dignified with impressive type in the telephone directory, but, whatever might be behind it, the façade of his Adam Street premises was of a less imposing character.

Billie came to a small, double-fronted shop, of which one window was no more than a large cage containing many small bright-plumaged birds which fluttered from perch to perch, making a movement which never ceased. The other showed a large tank, in which were strange fishes, newts, and aquatic plants—presumably such as were unattractive to the appetite of the water snake, four feet of sinuous olive-green, which swam monotonously round the sides of its narrow home.

There was nothing formidable in these exhibits, and Billie, pausing to inspect them before entering the shop, as a customer would be likely to do, was disposed to think that the importation of the wild fauna of South America was no more than a tradesman's brag, perhaps with no worse nor better object than to give dignity to the peddling of tortoises and tropic birds Or, with at least equal probability, to conceal activities of a less innocent nature.

Anyway, the name of M. Beal was over the door. There could be no doubt that this was the place, no doubt that its proprietor had been known to Mr. Catsgill as one on whose behalf the Mildew Gang would provide a very large sum to avert danger of his operations being betrayed to the police.

A bell clanged loudly as she pushed open the glass-panelled door and entered a dingy shop, the floor of which was strewn with sawdust, and the walls surrounded with cages, mostly empty, and the remainder containing nothing more formidable than a small cat-like creature with tufted ears.

She heard an approaching step, and, in the brief interval which passed before the inner door opened, she had a belated sense of the futility of what she did.

The attendant would tell her that he had nothing suitable to her requirements, or he would, more probably, press upon her some of the frowsy and repellent specimens of his meagre stock. She would refuse them and come out. What would she have done? What did she expect to be able to do? She most probably would not see Mr. Beal at all! The idea, which had appeared good in the vagueness of distance, shrank to truer proportions at a closer view.

The man who entered was repulsive rather than formidable. Elderly, though not old: so thin that his face appeared to be ridged with bones over which the skin was too tautly drawn. She was most conscious of yellow, broken teeth and of feet which shuffled along the ground. He was dirty, and his clothes looked suitable for the cleaning of cages, which may have been the occupation which filled his time.

He said, "Yes, ma'am?" in a vacuous manner, his eyes not falling directly upon her, so that Billie thought his interest in her to be less than she was giving to him. "I want some kind of a pet—a bird or animal, if you have anything suitable—for a wedding present. I want something that's not dangerous, of course, and clean in its habits, and not too difficult in the food it needs."

She spoke a formula which she had rehearsed. She thought it had a genuine sound; and it suggested a basis on which the relative suitability of various creatures might be discussed at length.

He answered vaguely: "I don't know. We don't do much in that way…. Perhaps I'd better tell Mr. Beal."

He turned as he spoke, and shuffled out of the shop.

Billie might claim that she had won the first trick, if not the game. She had put her request in such a form that she was likely to see the presumably criminal Beal, without having requested or shown any interest in his existence.

She might have felt some elation at that, but, in fact, she was conscious most of a desire to withdraw from the shop. It had an atmosphere which she did not like. Perhaps, she told herself, it was no more than a faint jungle-scent which still lingered around those wretched creatures brought to an alien land, to an existence of thwarted instincts and narrow bars, for the satisfaction of the curiosities of mankind. It is a sinister hostile scent, to which some people are particularly susceptible, while others do not perceive it at all.

But was it no more than that? What was it the man had said? "We don't do much in that way."

But what else should they be expected to do? She supposed (wrongly) that the main business of such a shop would be the sale of domestic pets. She judged, more accurately, that the stock she had yet seen did not indicate a trade which could support Mr. Beal and his shuffling assistant. But why should she jib at that? It only confirmed what had been expected before. It was an item of knowledge already gained, to be added to the mere address she had had from Mr. Catsgill, when she should inform the police, as she had little doubt that she would soon be doing. And when the proprietor should appear she could judge whether he were one who would be likely to live on the few pounds—shillings rather—that such a shop could provide.

Judging thus, on evidence which was misleading because still far from complete, she waited the long moment before Maurice Beal appeared, which he did so silently that she had no warning before the door opened to let him through. There might be no intention in that. He was one to whom quiet movement was as natural as to a jungle beast.

She saw a man scarcely as tall as herself, supple in movement, with black close-cut hair, and black, curiously opaque eyes. Their whites had a yellow tinge which matched the sallowness of his skin. He might drink at times, but it was a vice of which he showed no present sign. He was neatly dressed, and his clothes, of their kind, were good.

When he spoke, his English was carefully correct, though it had an accent he could not conceal. His voice was smooth, giving as much confidence as a leopard's purr. "You are enquiring," he asked, "for a lady's pet?"

"Yes," she answered, conscious of a violent beating of her heart which she could not check, and of an effort to control her voice, of the success of which she was not sure. "I thought of a small animal, or a bird."

"Bird? There are some in the window. Carl could have shown you those."

"I thought of something larger. Perhaps a parrot."

"Parrots are not popular as pets now. And there are difficulties about importation. Still, there are some available.... The present is for a friend?"

"It is to be a wedding gift."

"For which such a bird—"

She could not be sure whether the words were spoken half in earnest or wholly in jest. They came with no change of voice, and with a motion of the lips which showed white regular teeth, and was between a smile and a sneer. But she thought that if she had required a present for a successful rival in love, such as would be likely to give her a quick death, a parrot which had been in contact with the disease which can be so easily communicated to those who feed it would have been procurable for a sufficient price.

"No," she said, her lips forming a difficult smile, "I don't think I'd better choose a parrot, if they are not safe.... I suppose monkeys are rather out of your line?"

"Oh no. I have plenty of them. You mustn't judge the stock from this shop. There's no room to show it here. And, besides, almost all our business is done by mail. It isn't often that a lady like you—you'd better come through and see."

She knew why she had been frightened now. As he had looked at her his eyes had rested a moment upon her chin, where a bruise she had taken from Mr. Wellard's hand was still faintly visible. Instinct, sounder than reason, told her that he had recognized who she was. Reason, claiming control, told her that it was a cowardly, unfounded fear. How should he know anything of her at all? Why should there have been the remotest reason to suppose that she would be calling here? But for that whispered word in Mr. Catsgill's office there would not have been one millionth chance that she would ever have entered the shop. And was it not natural for the eyes of anyone who looked at her face to notice so plain a bruise? It would be a source of lasting self-contempt if she should fail to master this silly fear.

She followed him up two flights of a narrow stair, the jungle odour becoming stronger as she climbed. At the second landing they turned into a long passage, giving her the first intimation that the extent of Mr. Beal's premises was not disclosed by the shop through which she had entered. They passed a door through which came sounds of snarling and of some great creature bounding about, and when they came out on to a narrow wooden bridge with a paved yard below them, littered with packing-cases, upon which two carpenters were working with noises of hammer and saw, Billie, looking down, felt some return of confidence, as illogical as her former fear. For nearly two thousand years carpenters have been regarded as particularly innocent men.

"We do all the wholesale business, and that with the larger animals, from the Trevor Street entrance. There wouldn't be room for them to pass through the shop door," Mr. Beal's voice purred at her side. Why should he tell her that? It might be natural enough but she felt the tone to be that of one who soothes a nervous beast into a cage. He was only talking to occupy her mind as he led her on! But her reason asked: Was it not your purpose in coming here to get him to talk? When he does so, will you let the conversation fail because of your silly fears?"

"I suppose," she said, "you supply zoological gardens and places like those?"

"Yes," he assented, "and we import thousands of monkeys for vivisection every year. That's the most regular part of the business. We've just executed the largest order for Berlin that we've ever had. And, of course, other creatures. We've got a special order now for seven hundred female rats, to be guaranteed healthy, and not more than six weeks old."

"Rats?" she exclaimed, with repulsion and fear evident in her voice. She had a horror of a single rat. Seven hundred at once!

"Oh," he assured her soothingly, "we shan't go near any of them. Not if you come this way."

They had crossed the bridge and descended a flight of stairs in the Trevor Street premises now, and approached a door very solidly made, inset with thick plate glass, which was covered with heavy wire netting on the inner side. He looked carefully through this glass before unlocking the door, and had he made the normal gesture of politeness which would have invited her to enter first she might have hesitated, but he led the way, and that, with the assurance he had just given that the direction they took would avoid the rats, caused her to follow him readily into what, as she looked round, had the appearance of an empty cage with a heap of loose straw on the floor. She was more conscious, as she entered, of humid heat than of anything that she saw.

He closed the door behind her, stepped quickly across the cage, unlocked another similarly glazed and wired on the further side, and then, instead of holding it open for her to follow, swung it so that it closed in her face.

"Mr. Beal," she called, in the first futile burst of anger and fear, "what do you mean? Open the door! It's not the kind of joke—"

He raised his voice slightly, that it might penetrate through the small sliding ventilation panel which he pushed open, but otherwise spoke without any evidence of emotion as he replied: "Miss Wingrove, if I were in your place I shouldn't make so much noise. If you look on the other side of the cage you'll see that you're not alone.

It's asleep now, but, if you wake it, I might not be able to save you, even if I should try, which I should see little reason to do."

She followed his eyes, and saw, with a thrill of horror, a huge snake curled up on the other side of the straw. Its head was cushioned on its coils. Its eyes were closed. Its tale twitched slightly as she looked, as though it were near to wake.

"I must ask you a few questions," her captor went on, "and it will depend on how you answer them when you come out, or whether you come out at all.

"Perhaps it may assist you to a greater candour if you understand exactly what your companion is. It is an anaconda, the kind of snake frequently, but quite erroneously, called a boa constrictor in this country.

"The boa constrictor is actually quite small, rarely exceeding ten feet in length, and is frequently tamed, being useful for catching rats. I have myself seen and handled such specimens in villages in the Amazon basin. I have seen children with them curled playfully round their necks.

"But the anaconda is untameable. The one you see reached this country a few weeks ago. When last measured it was thirty-two feet three inches long. It could swallow an ox. It is now sleeping off the effect of such a meal. When it wakes, which may not be for one or two further days, or any moment now, it will be hungry for the next.

"You will see the importance of remaining quiet, and you will also recognize the advantage it would be to me to go away and forget you are here. Your companion is destined for the Amsterdam Zoo, if we can agree upon the price, concerning which a little difference has arisen. Meanwhile I have to feed it, at intervals of some weeks it is true, but it is difficult to satisfy it at a cost of less than six or eight pounds.

"You will save me that sum if you remain here, and you will observe that it is a method of disposing of you by which the greatest difficulty of such transactions—the removal of the dead body—does not arise."

CHAPTER X.

A Conversation Under Difficulties

BILLIE heard the animal dealer's cynical threat, and became curiously aware that her heart was no longer beating with an uncomfortable rapidity. She had become quietly but most alertly conscious of her surroundings. Her thoughts had become supernormally clear. She had always had an intense horror of snakes, but that appeared to be in abeyance now. All feeling, all emotion, seemed to be suspended by the danger in which she stood. As she heard the final suggestion that, if she were devoured by the snake, there would be nothing left to conceal, there came a memory of having read that this class of reptile disgorges the skeleton and other indigestible parts of his victim—surely in a form by which the original structure could be identified! But even this imagination did not stir her to any extremity of horror or fear. She said boldly: "It isn't true."

He shook his head: "I can't hear, unless you talk more loudly than that."

She repeated the words in raised voice.

His answer showed that he had followed her thought. "Oh, the furnace would deal with that."

She thought: "If I go on shouting I may rouse the snake. On the other hand, if I refuse to speak he may go, and, before he does that, he may rouse it himself. I don't think I'm going to be killed here. I think that Eustace will come in time. Or the police. But, meanwhile, if I can keep him talking—" She asked boldly: "What do you want me to say?"

As she asked the question, though she did not move her eyes, her mind searched the cage for any place at which she could break out if he were to go. But she was not hopeful of that. Anything beyond the anaconda's strength would be beyond hers. Any hole which would be too small for it would be too small for her.

51

There was a tank of warm water on the further side, which explained the humidity of the air. There was the heaped straw on the floor. Rising from floor to roof there was the great branching limb of a dead tree. Otherwise there was nothing there. Nothing from which a weapon could be contrived. She had an irrelevant but correct idea that the cage was not originally intended for such an inmate, but rather for some large predatory beast.

Could she grasp its comparatively slender neck and break it before it should wake? She thought not. She considered that while there is a measure of security to be gained by grasping the neck of a poisonous snake, there is little gain in such a hold upon one which can wrap itself round you in constricting bone-breaking coils. No, her security was to talk, to obey, to hope that the snake's torpor would last, and, if it did not, perhaps, for a time—if she lay down—if she were still.

All these thoughts came and passed, as she asked that question, "What do you want me to say?" and heard his reply: "I want you to tell me why you came here."

What was the object in lying now? The truth might be the safer as well as the simpler path.

But, as she thought this, an idea came. She said: "To see you, of course."

"Why?"

"To give you a chance of saving your own skin by giving information to the police." That was certainly not what he had expected to hear. He blinked uneasily before he gathered boldness to answer: "That's nonsense. You wouldn't have come the way you did."

"You don't know how I came. You think I'm in danger now, when it's really you."

This was not exactly the path of simple rectitude which she had intended to tread. Rather it was bluff answering bluff, with truth a casual, disregarded ingredient in whatever it might seem expedient to declare.

He looked at her with evil eyes, but she saw that she had caused him at least a moment of indecision. Then he said: "You're doing yourself no good. If you want to get out alive you'll have to talk a lot plainer than that."

"I'll talk plainly enough if you'll let me out. I shan't say more while I'm shut in here."

He considered this in an evident doubt. He thought of a test question, which might reveal much, indirectly, both of her veracity and of the measure of danger in which he lay. "If you'll tell me," he said, "who gave you my name, and why, we'll finish this talk in another place."

She saw afterwards that she could have given many answers—anything but the truth—which would have freed her from the peril in which she stood. She might have said she had his name from Wellard, from Mildew. She might have made up any one of a score of specious explanations that would have been sufficient to rouse his curiosity or his fear, and sounded sufficiently plausible for belief. But her first thought was that he had asked the one thing she must not tell, and on that she replied: "I shouldn't tell you, even if you did let me out. It's something you've no business to know."

"Then," he said, "you can just stay where you are." He turned with the words, and in an instant she was alone with that sleeping death....

Leaving her thus, he walked quickly away, gnawing his lip. He was frightened and not sure that he had not acted a fool's part. If the girl had come on her own, it was a case for getting all possible information from her, and then disposing of her in such a manner that she would not be heard of again. He was not sure that the anaconda would be the best method for that, nor did he think her to be in imminent danger. The creature might rouse itself any moment, or it might lie there for another week. You could never tell. But it was a risk which she must take. He had other matters upon his mind, which were more important to him.

He must ascertain, first, whether she had come alone, whether the place were watched. It might be prudent to make report, to obtain instructions. Not that he considered himself to be subordinate to anyone. No one else could do what he did. He would be almost impossible to replace. His position was impregnable, *so long as he should not be suspected by the police*. But if it should happen, his importance would be over, his use done. His life, if Mildew considered the fault were his, might not endure for an hour. He used his private telephone first, which penetrated the ramifications of his rather extensive premises, including communication with some that were two streets away.

When he had done that, he felt assured that there would be no police intrusions upon him without the notice he required; sure, if they should enter, that there would be diversions, such as an escaped and (presumably) poisonous reptile to delay their penetration of his peculiar premises. That provision having been made, he rang up a number which he always carried in his mind, and indulged in an apparently innocent conversation, the substance of which would (as he correctly supposed) be relayed to another number he did not know, though he knew much. He had mentioned, among other things, having on his premises the animal with the damaged jaw, and raised the question of whether it would be profitable to keep it longer alive.

CHAPTER XI.

The Indifference of Superintendent Backwash

EUSTACE sat in a teashop in Whitechapel Road for forty minutes, as he had agreed to do. He could see the end of Adam Street, round the corner of which Billie had said she would come on her way to the bus which she was to board without waiting for him, lest their meeting should be observed. He kept his eyes continually on this spot, first in fairly confident anticipation, and then in steadily increasing anxiety as the time lengthened. But for forty minutes he did not move.

That had been the bargain which they had agreed to observe.

That seemed to allow an ample margin for any innocent reception that she might meet. He had thought five or ten minutes to be a more probable limit.

And their final bargain had been that the police might be informed by him under such circumstances without an inexcusable breach of her own promise, on which he had given his even more reluctant pledge that he would not enter the shop until official assistance had been obtained. For no very logical reason they had even compared their watches before they parted.

For the last five minutes he sat with his own before him, his eyes falling continually upon the movement of the second hand, and lifting again lest he should fail to see her as she came round the corner.

Would she, he asked himself, if all were well, go so near to the agreed limit, reluctant for him to call in the police as he knew her to be—an inclination which might not be lessened if she were successful in what she did? Well, she might. She might have engaged herself in a conversation she was reluctant to close. She would be cool and exact, and rely on him for the same qualities. Till the last second passed he could neither abandon hope that she would appear, nor break faith with her.

But he lost no second beyond. At the stroke of the bargained time his check was already paid, and he was on the way to a telephone box fifty yards up the street, which he had located previously.

As he approached it a man who looked as though his time were normally spent between lamp post and bar made a quick movement to enter before him. Eustace, already moving rapidly, made an extra spurt, so that their shoulders jostled at the door of the box.

"Pardon me," he said, declining to give way, "a matter of urgency."

"No you don't, mate. I wor first here," the man answered roughly. His shoulder pushed Eustace aside.

A suspicion that this was no chance obstruction came to his mind. If that were so, it was no time for persuasive words, and Billie's peril might be desperate indeed. With all the force of the anger and fear that this thought aroused, he drove his fist at the man's chin, and saw him go down on his back as he pushed into the booth.

Heedless of the little crowd that gathered instantly round the sprawling form, until the sight of an approaching constable caused it to rise in haste and disappear in the opposite direction, he dialled 1212, and had no cause to complain that he was not instantly heard. "Scotland Yard," he said. "It's a matter of life and death."

A moment later he was put through. "I want Inspector Cauldron," he said. "It's a most urgent matter."

"I don't know that he's about now," an alert but unexcited voice answered. "If it's so urgent, you'd better tell me what it is."

"I want 4, Adam Street, Whitechapel, raided at once. Tell him that Miss Wingrove is caught in there. If he's not about, let Superintendent Backwash know. He'd do just as well."

"Yes, I suppose he would." There was the faintest trace of sarcasm in the reply. "And who shall I say you are?"

"Eustace Limbrook."

"Wait a moment."

There was not long to wait. Probably the whole time had not been thirty seconds before he heard the superintendent's voice: "Yes? That Mr. Limbrook? Where are you speaking from?"

"A phone box in the Whitechapel Road."

"And what the hell are you doing there?"

"There's not time to explain. We're on the track of the Mildew Gang from a new angle. What I want you to know is that Miss Wingrove has disappeared in one of their dens—4, Adam Street, close to here—and it needs raiding at once."

"Why do you say she's disappeared?"

Hurriedly, but clearly enough, he gave an account of the position, omitting only the source from which the name of the wild-animal dealer had been obtained.

In his own office Superintendent Backwash listened without interruption. At its conclusion he looked across at a stenographer at another instrument. "Got that, Pearson?"

"Yes, sir."

He addressed himself to his own mouthpiece.

"Sorry, Mr. Limbrook, but we can't raid a respectable rate-payer's premises on no better pretext than that. I expect Miss Wingrove's been detained a few minutes longer than she expected, or gone home a different way. If ladies did no more foolish things than that, we should have an easier time.

"If you call at the shop you'll find her chatting there, or learn that she left ten minutes ago, more likely than not. If she's not home when you get back, you can call us up, and we'll send an officer round, but I don't think you'll find there'll be any need for that."

"But, Superintendent...."

"Sorry, Mr. Limbrook. I'm extremely busy. We told you to stay in Scotland, and if you won't take our advice you must manage your own affairs in your own way."

With these words he hung up before there could be time for any reply. For perhaps fifteen seconds he sat in what appeared to be a half-somnolent state. His thought was: "I'm not sure yet whether it was the worst day of my life or the best when Cauldron arrested a man we'd no business to touch; but today it's going to be a rise or resignation for me. There's no time for consultation. And if I asked for authority for what I'm going to do, I shouldn't get it, more likely than not.

"Phone for Cauldron. He's to come here the first moment he can.... I want Inspectors Pearce and Baker here for instructions at once.... Tell Jeeves to have his raiding squad ready to start in four minutes from now. Yes. Armed."

He picked up his own receiver again. He gave the names of the three police stations nearest to the Whitechapel Road. "Get me through to them.... No, instantly! Damn the Towcaster call. Mullins, you're doing your little bit in the biggest coup or the worst cropper we ever made."

A moment later he had ordered that an enquiry as to Mr. Cats-gill's condition should be put through to the West London Hospital. Then he spoke rapidly to the chiefs of the three police stations he had called, and sat back for another moment of thought.

"An importer of wild animals!" he was saying to himself as Inspector Cauldron entered the room. "Could anything be more obvious? And even after those Syrian bibles, Cauldron, we never had the gumption to think of that...! What's the matter? Oh, I want you to fetch Mildew in. It doesn't matter what for. We just want to see him, but *make him come*. And no communications with anyone first. Everything's in the surprise, and I'm not sure that I'm not too late. I'm just gambling on that. And have his house searched and his correspondence sealed up. And have every telephone call that comes through for him recorded and traced to its source. Don't lose a moment. I'll leave that angle absolutely to you.... What other angle is there? Why, that Wingrove girl has held the key to the whole problem in her exasperating little head all the time, and now very likely got beaten up, if not killed, in giving them the warning that may blow the whole thing out.

"Ever thought of the false bottom of a snake's or puma's cage for hiding dope where no one would be likely to go scratching about? Well, someone else has, and I'm going to prove that, or write my resignation within a week.

"I can see now that, if we'd had the sense to take Catsgill's tip, we should have been running up the flag before this. I only hope it's not too late yet.

"Want to handle the raid? Yes, of course. But you can't. I'm going to do that myself. If you get Mildew—by the way, don't let him shoot himself, he's just the sort to try that if he thinks he's caught—if you get him with the evidence on him, so to speak, you'll have done your share.... I can't stop for a word more now.... Pearce, and you, Baker—I want you to come with me."

As he spoke he pulled open a drawer of his desk and transferred its contents to his pockets, which bulged responsively; and then, with an agility of movement surprising in so heavy a man, and which, in fact, he seldom displayed, he led them out of the room.

CHAPTER XII.

SOME LIES TO DELAY DEATH

LEFT alone with her thoughts and the sleeping snake, Billie considered what she should do, imagined many things, and actually did nothing (which may have been wisest of all) until Mr. Beal appeared again in little more than five minutes, though it seemed longer to her.

She had considered the contents of her handbag, and found nothing more helpful there than a thin card of cigarette matches. She had read that all wild creatures are afraid of fire, and if an anaconda be an exception to this rule it is a fact which the natural history books do not stress. Yet when she compared the relative size of the snake and of the seven matches she had, it was difficult to nourish a sanguine hope that they would be an enduring shield.

She had a brighter but yet no more than a flickering hope when she reflected that even the smallest match might ignite straw. Suppose she should pile it between herself and the snake, and light it as soon as direction? But suppose that it would not be the anaconda but she who would succumb, if not to the roasting heat, to the smoke fumes in that ill-ventilated cage?

As to that, might she not protect herself by creeping into the water tank? She had read of men who had saved their lives from prairie fire by lying in a little stream with their faces uncovered only so far as breathing required.

But suppose, again, that the anaconda should have the same idea? There was enough space in the tank for her to immerse herself in the warm water. There might even be sufficient for the anaconda to do so, though she was less certain of that. But there would certainly not be room for both, even had they been congenial companions for a watery bed.

She had a disconcerting imagination of the great snake putting two or three feet of sinuous muscular neck beneath her, to heave her out of the tank and on to the burning straw. She must think of something better than that.

Probably the best thing was to do nothing. To remain quiescent, remembering that time would be in her favour. Rescue could hardly be long delayed. And if she should remain still—perhaps lying under the straw—the snake might not be in haste to molest her.

She had coolness and wit enough to see that the idea which Mr. Beal had given her of a creature waking hungry for an instant meal could scarcely be literal fact. For, if so, it would do nothing but swallow and sleep, wake, and swallow, and sleep again. A dull—it might even be called an impossible—life.

More probably the digestion of the heavy meal would be followed by an interval of active well-being before hunger would become urgent again. Yes, but "active." It was her own word, and still one that she did not like. For the first time her imagination gave her a vision of that thirty-two-feet length of gliding flexible muscle moving quickly in the narrow space, with a vividness at which panic came. so that she must restrain herself with difficulty from beating upon the thick wire meshing between her and the plate glass that would be easier to break.

She must not think of that! Must believe that the huge snake would sleep until help should come.... She saw Beal at the door.

"Miss Wingrove," he said, "I've got an offer to make, and it's your last chance. It's no good telling me that the police are anywhere here about, because I know they are not. But if you can prove to me that they know you're here—that they are smelling round and will make trouble if they don't see you again—then I'll come to terms with you and them, and tell them all that I know.

"But if not—well, you brought it on yourself when you came here, as though you thought we were fools.... So it's for you to say your piece now, and you know best what your life's likely to be worth when it's been said."

"I shan't say anything while I'm shut up here. I'm not afraid. I've no doubt I shall live a lot longer than you."

"If you've nothing more to say than that I shall poke the snake up and leave you to talk it over with him."

She was not sufficiently sure that this threat was bluff to receive it with a quiet mind, nor was she confident of her power to convince with what must have been more or less an impromptu lie, unless it should disclose the part which Eustace was playing, which she was resolved, at whatever cost, that she would not do.

She played a better card when she retorted: "If you do, you'll lose it. I should have thought it was worth a good bit."

Mr. Beal's teeth showed in an angry smile. "I'm not afraid of any damage you'll be able to do."

"Then that shows what a fool you are. I shall light the straw."

The sneer left his face as she said this, and gave place to an obvious disquietude. The anaconda was worth a large sum. It was a variety of snake for which there was always a good market, even when, as was usual with imported specimens, they were only young ones, five or ten feet in length. The existence of such monsters as the present specimen was well enough known. There were stuffed ones in the European museums. But the difficulties of capture and transportation of the full-grown snake, as they exist in the remote immensities of the Amazonian swamps, are of a prohibitive kind. The present specimen was hard to value. The offer which he was hesitating to accept was £700, with all expenses paid from the moment when the drugged monster had been passed down, yard by yard, like a huge cable, into the hold of an ancient paddle-wheel cargo boat, moored to a wooden pier on a tributary of the Upper Amazon, two thousand miles from the sea.

And, besides its actual value, there was another consideration. It is not only men of simple and upright character who have pride in business prestige. Maurice Beal had the reputation of being the leading dealer in South American fauna throughout the world. His agencies extended into the remotest swamps, the most inaccessible mountain ranges, of the least-known portion of our half-populated world. It was his boast that there was no living product of that mysterious continent, plant or insect, bird or animal, which he could not supply for a proper price. The present importation had attracted attention in zoological circles throughout the world. It had immensely raised his prestige. It would be a wretched conclusion to have to announce that it had been accidentally destroyed (and even the skin might be injured beyond repair!), and it was all through the carelessness of putting it there to sleep off its last meal without removing the straw, which is out of place in a reptile's pen.

He said savagely: "You won't do that. You'd get roasted yourself."

She smiled confidently, seeing the effect of her threat. "I don't think I should. I know how to manage better than that." She tried to drive home a success she had already won, and said a word too many. "I'll just tell you this before you open the door. The police will be here within an hour of when I came, if I'm not away before then."

His eyes fell to a watch, smaller than is usually worn by men, which was set in Brazilian diamonds on his brown wrist. "So that's it, is it?" he said. "Then we've got plenty of time. We'd better clear matters up before they come smelling round."

Her eyes fell to her own wrist. Was it possible? Had the watch stopped? No, it ticked steadily on. It was just twenty-two minutes since she had parted with Eustace in the Whitechapel Road. He would still be sitting there watching for her appearance at the street corner. Actually, the time had not yet come when he would place his own watch before him, and set his eyes on the interminable slowness with which the second hand circled its tiny dial. Thirty-eight minutes to go! And even that was a sanguine estimate. How could she be sure that any help would arrive within twenty minutes of when Eustace would feel free to raise an alarm? She had simply warned the man to get rid of her before any help could possibly appear!

Maurice Beal unlocked the door. "Come out!" he said curtly.

Playing desperately for time, she made no advance.

"I'm not sure," she said, "that I'm not best where I am. I'm not sure that I don't like the snake better than you."

He made no answer, except to pull a whistle from his vest pocket and blow a shrill call, on which two men came at a run.

He said something to one which she could not hear, at which he went. To the other—a man darker and of even more dubious ancestry than himself, he said: "Get her out of there."

"You needn't trouble," she said, "I'm coming now." She stepped forward, and, as she did so, threw a lighted match into the straw. That would give them something to think about besides her!

Beal's voice lost all its smoothness as he yelled: "Put it out, Pedro! Put it out!" But he did not therefore take his attention from her. He gripped her arm as she tried to slip past, and she learnt his strength. It would have been as easy to break from a wire rope.

He held her thus while, for some brief moments, Pedro stamped on the straw. At one moment it seemed to be out, and then it flickered again.

Beal looked anxious. He was neither willing to loose her nor to watch the flame gaining strength. He saw that the great snake had begun to move. He dragged her back to the cage. She struggled vainly, terrified of what he might be meaning to do.

He gave a jeering laugh. "She lit it," he said. "She's the one who should put it out." Together the two men rolled her over, pressing her down on the smouldering straw. Her dress caught as they did this, but was smothered in turn. Next moment they were out of the cage. The great snake, wide awake now, was writhing in panic at its further side.

Along the passage she saw the other man returning. Behind him a jaguar walked, unleashed, on noiseless feet, its head low.

Beal loosed his grip on her arm. "You can run now if you like," he said. "But it won't be far." He looked at the beast, which was now rubbing his leg, with a loud purr. It was a hint which she could not miss.

"Another failure," she thought, looking at the extinguished straw, and down at her own dress, which was brown cinder at one side, likely to flake away at a touch. But she looked at her watch again, and was less sure. Another four minutes was gone. Eustace would soon be doing something now!

Beal led the way to his own office. He sat down at his desk, pointing her to a chair at its opposite side. He sent the two men away. The jaguar lay at his right hand, its head on its paws. Its yellow eyes were fixed upon her.

"Miss Wingrove," he said, "you can't expect that I shall let you live after what I've heard from you, and what's happened now. If you've told me the truth, and the police come, they will learn that you called and went away.

"If they search they will find nothing, unless events should have moved in such a direction that you will have been killed by my little friend here, as is liable to happen to anyone who makes an unauthorized intrusion into my private office, and for which I could not be greatly blamed. The only objection to that is that the police would probably want to shoot her, which I should not willingly permit. She was a cub when I picked her up in Ecuador, and is, in all ways, the best friend I have.

"Now, Miss Wingrove, the time is short. I want you to tell me how you got this address, why you came here, and—in fact, all you can. You'll have five minutes for that.

"If you play fair I shall either come to terms with you, or give you a drug which will make the whole thing quite a pleasant experience—a good deal more so than you deserve.

"If you won't speak, or I catch you out in a lie, you'll be taken down to the shop where they cut up the meat for feeding the beasts, and the butcher there will skin you before you die, or as much of you as time will safely allow.

"You have never seen that done? So I supposed. Neither have I, except the left arm. But that was very interesting to watch. It is an experience which you will do well to avoid.

"Now tell me. Who sent you here...? If you move the Holy Virgin will spring. She won't kill you. Don't hope that. She'll hold you down till I decide what to do next."

"You call that beast that?"

"Yes. It's a very suitable name. It's a better character than most Christians, and otherwise answers the description better than most of them would. But don't waste time, for my patience will soon be gone."

But to waste time was just what Billie was desperately determined to do. She asked: "If I tell you, how do I know that you'll keep faith?"

"You don't. You risk that. But it's a promise I've no reason to break. I've no quarrel with you, if you help me, though it may be foolish to let you live."

"I'll tell you what I can," Billie lied, still fencing for time, and fearing most of all what would happen if she should faint—perhaps to lose a consciousness which would not be allowed to return. "When I've done that, you won't want to kill me. You'll be anxious to save yourself, and glad of any help I can give. The trouble is that, if you want it all in five minutes, I don't know where to begin."

"You'd better begin somewhere, and sharp "

"Well, I suppose you know where Mr. Mildew is?"

"I may. What of that?"

"Well, I wasn't sure. He's been rather clever at keeping himself back, so that if there's any hanging or going to jail it can be done by others instead of him."

"Hanging?" Beal scowled. "There's been no question of that. You don't know the English law."

"Oh, I do! It's funny. It makes it just as bad to kill the worst traitor in a criminal gang as—well, say the Prime Minister's wife! But, anyway, you don't know what Mr. Mildew said."

"You mean Mildew gave me away?"

"Yes, of course."

Heaven help her invention now! Distrusting what it might be equal to do at this sudden call—for it was only as the words came that she had thought of imputing to the gang leader something which he had not happened to do—she took refuge on an island of truth.

"I'd better tell you how it began." She narrated how Eustace had been used to get the drugs through the Customs, the curious accident of his arrest, and how his statement to the police had brought Cornelius Mildew under suspicion.

As she told this tale she saw that she was believed and that she had won his attention, so that, for some brief moments, he forgot the passage of time. But she could not hope that that obliviousness would endure. Unless she could persuade him to let her live, each minute must make the crisis more imminent, the peril greater. And but for that crouching beast she might have made an effort to escape even now. She was much nearer the door. She could be outside before Beal could possibly get over or round his desk. And in the corner near the door was a knobbed stick, which looked heavy and hard. Even a woman, fighting for life, might do something with that.

It was the jaguar which made her pause. She had kept her eyes upon it, meeting its own while she talked, and had had the satisfaction of seeing it blink uneasily, as though soul met soul, and it knew its inferiority stood revealed.

But she had not been trying to stare it down. She had been wondering whether there were no bridge of understanding that could make friendship of what lay beneath the flattened skull and behind those yellow, inscrutable eyes. Some thoughts the creature must have. Some lonely incommunicable thoughts. But what meeting-ground could there be beyond that of a common sex? Kipling's line, "Nay, we be women together," came whimsically to her mind, as so much had come in the last half hour, which might be said to be the first she had fully lived.

"Mr. Mildew," she went on, "when Inspector Cauldron called on him, and he found they knew more than he could hope to deny, offered to give them information against you and a lot of other people, if they would let him go free. I believe they promised this, more or less, but only if what he told them was true, and they're not sure that it was."

"What did he say about me?"

"That you're the real head of the gang."

She saw, as she said it, that it was not what he had expected, or feared, to hear. Evidently there was something he was, or did, that something, probably, which made him invaluable to the gang, which she should be able to mention. She saw the doubt in his eyes. And to save her life—literally to save her life!—she could not guess what it might be.

She went on talking at random, to give her mind time for that desperate quest. "But before I tell you what I've really come here to say, you ought to know that I'm not saying it because I feel I'm in your power at all. I don't believe that leopard, or whatever it is, would do me any harm if you told it to, which I'm quite certain you won't. It knows I'm—another woman—and we've been making friends all the time I've been sitting here."

He stared at that, and then gave a short laugh, which was not pleasant to hear. "So you count on that, do you? You think bitches all hold together? You don't know that any of them will do more for a man than for any of their sex that they ever met? If you're as silly as that, it's no wonder you've got yourself into this mess here.... But if you want me to think you've been telling the truth, you'd better explain why, if the police know such a hell of a lot, you came here alone in the way you did."

It was the suggestion her imagination required. It brought back the idea which had lain at her mind's door when she had talked of hanging a few minutes earlier.

"Yes," she answered confidently. "That's just what I've been wanting to tell you. Mr. Mildew said that when any of the gang didn't give satisfaction you were the one who did him in. I think that's the right expression. He gave the police a list of the people he said you'd killed. But, of course, saying that isn't proof, and they don't know what to believe.

"They thought, if they sent any one of themselves here, you'd be sure to know him, so it was arranged that I should go away to Scotland, and then come secretly back, and call on you the way I have, and see what I could.

"Of course, if you were silly enough to try doing me any harm, it would just prove to the police that everything Mildew said about you is true. But if it isn't, and you can tell them a better tale, you might get him where he's tried to put you. You'll see, if you think it out, that treating me well means as much to you as to me, with the police watching to see what will happen the way they are."

Billie stopped, somewhat out of breath with the effort of this culminating mendacity, and perhaps with anxiety also, for she had been watching his face, and its emotions were plain to read, and of doubtful import for her.

She did not doubt that he believed; nor did she doubt that, whatever other services he might have rendered the gang, he had been the instrument by which those whom it condemned had come to a quick end. His eyes had been venomous, but not indignant, as he had heard that accusation against himself. But her concluding words left him silent, looking at her in doubt, while he gnawed his lip. Had he treated her in a different way—had he not left her in the anaconda's cage? Yet he had had cause to think her a spy. And the police would not be asked to believe him a saint, but only one who would save himself by giving others away. So he hesitated. But when the decision came she saw in his eyes, before he spoke, that it would not be hopeful for her.

"Miss Wingrove," he said, "I don't say that all you've told me's not true, and I'm sorry I can't let you go. But I didn't promise that, and the risk's too big. All the same, if you make no trouble for us, we shan't make much for you. It will just be something to drink, and be over as quick as that."

He snapped his fingers to indicate the ease and rapidity of her exit from earthly life.

CHAPTER XIII.

Mr. Beal Takes a Softer Seat

THE utterly unexpected event will either stimulate or stun the mind, according to its own nature, and that upon which its impact comes. No response to Eustace's plea for police assistance could have been more unexpected than that which he received from Superintendent Backwash—it is a tribute to the thoroughness of that most capable officer's methods that the idea of finesse did not enter his head—and its effect was to rouse him to a coldly indignant determination that he would attempt his sister's rescue without regard for other consequences, and to the confusion of the C.I.D.

It would be an inaccuracy of diagnosis to conclude that he would not otherwise have made that desperate attempt, but it would have been in a different mood. He would have been more conscious of its difficulties, more dubious of its success. Now, in his bitter reaction to that repulse, he felt indifferent to consequence, and, as he believed that he could rely less on others, he became more sure of himself.

When, in South America, he had been in control of some hundreds of workmen of diverse breeds, he had been advised to carry a revolver, which he had worn, conspicuously enough, in the hip pocket, which had been exposed by the undress of a tropic climate.

It was a weapon which he had never had occasion to put to serious use, and his trials of it had been limited to a few shots at a cardboard target, which he had not always contrived to hit. It was only since he had left the security of a prison cell, and had realized that life may, for some, be as hazardous in a civilized country as in Uruguayan wilds, that he had returned it to its usual pocket, where it had been less conspicuous now that he was more fully clothed than the conveniences or conventions of tropic climates require. Almost furtively, before setting out, he had slipped in the cartridges while Bil-

68

lie had been occupied in the adjoining bathroom, telling himself that she must not be alarmed by the implications of what he did, but with a basic hatred of melodrama inclining him to this reticence quite as much as consideration for her.

Now, as he walked hurriedly back toward Adam Street, he took out the weapon, without a thought of who might observe the action in the crowded thoroughfare, and transferred it to a jacket pocket, where it could be reached that half-second sooner which may be of vital importance when occasions of violence arise.

When he entered the shop, he encountered the same man who had appeared when Billie had clanged the bell. But on this occasion there was no waiting for him to obey its summons. He stood by the door at the back of the shop, scraping an empty cage.

"I want," Eustace said, in a voice which he modulated with difficulty, so that it was not free from a minatory sound, "to see the lady who called here an hour ago."

"The lady, sir?" the man echoed vaguely, and then added: "You'll wish to see Mr. Beal, sir. Yes, sir. Come this way."

He turned to the door as he spoke, and Eustace might have been content to follow where he led, but at that instant, in the reflection of a glass-backed tank, he saw the loiterer who had attempted to prevent him entering the telephone booth. He stood outside the shop door and was gesticulating to the man within.

There was no time to analyze the significance of this incident, but a realization of its sinister implications, and perhaps an association of ideas, as the man's face recalled the memory of how he had been upset by one successful blow, caused an instinctive action which cooler reflection might have found it hard to justify.

With no premonitory indication of coming violence, he struck suddenly upward at the chin of the elderly inoffensive shopman who was about to guide him through the door. The blow was as decisive as had been the one which suggested it to his mind. The man went backward. His head struck, and broke, the glass tank which had mirrored the warning signal. He fell and lay, his head bleeding freely, less damaged by the blow than by the cuts of the broken glass.

"Thank you," Eustace said, as he struck, "I'd rather find my own way." He had a moment's consciousness of the man whom he had seen in the street rushing in, with a fresh clamour of the bell, and then he was through the inner door, groping for a bolt which he was fortunate to find, and driving it in as the handle was seized and shaken violently on the other side.

He saw that now, even should he find Mr. Beal by his unaided effort, the occasion was not likely to be one of a friendly talk, nor could he reasonably hope for anything better than that Billie might still be an uninjured prisoner in this half-lighted, foul-smelling den.

To explore swiftly, to use every moment that might still be unopposed, was the obvious course to take. He looked into a rear room, dimly lit and shuttered. There was no time to be wasted there.

He hesitated between the foot of the narrow stairs and the cellar door, but decided in favour of the ascent. Should he enter the cellar, he might find himself trapped in a place from which he could not return. The upper rooms would be more numerous, lighter, in every way the better to be first explored.

So far he had no adequate idea of the extent of the premises, which were entered on the one side from the dingy shop. He paused on the first landing, shook three locked doors which gave no response except that there came from one an animal snarl, and went up again to a landing, where he wasted no time on the closed doors, seeing the bridge which had been thrown across to the opposite premises, and thinking, with an instant certainty: "She is not here. They will have taken her over there."

He thought as he ran over the bridge: "I shall be lucky if I find her alive. Luckier still if we get out of here, and both live…. But it is Superintendent Backwash's fault. He will have a bad time when he knows what his refusal has cost."

He had a queer undercurrent of satisfaction in that idea of the superintendent's belated and vain regrets; and, with it, a sense of primitive freedom, as of one who, by implication, had been told to take the law into his own hands. For if the police be told of abductions, murders, and rapes, and reply that it is not their business to interfere, what else will be the reasonable result?

It was true, in prosaic fact, that he had reported no more to Scotland Yard than that his sister had left him to make a call, and had failed to meet him thereafter with promised promptitude, but he was not in the mood for a cool exactness which, after all, would have been less than just to the real problem he had to face.

He drew the revolver from his pocket, unaware that he was prompted to that display even more by the faint jungle odour which was round him on every side than by the errand on which he came.

He ran down one set of stairs and came to a long passage, with windows on one side, and doors on the other. There was a shorter passage at right angles, the floor of which was linoleumed, whereas that of the longer one was bare. Offices, he judged, in one direction, and warehouses, perhaps pens for living stock, in the other.

"I want," he thought, "to find Billie, not to talk to Beal." He chose the longer passage.

He shook three locked doors and opened a fourth which he closed again in haste, and with a sense that long-tailed monkeys were leaping around his head.

As he drew back a man came out of the next door, a pitchfork in his hand. "Hey, you!" he said, "what are you doing there?"

"I'm looking for a lady who's somewhere here. If you can tell me where she is, I'll give you five pounds."

"You'd better come to the guv'nor and talk to him."

The man, who looked to be of a dull but dangerous disposition, advanced upon him with the pitchfork threateningly forward. He stopped at the sight of the lifted revolver and the sharp command: "Don't come nearer. I shall fire if you do." And then: "Drop it! Drop it, if you value your life. You'll get a bullet quicker than you can throw."

The man, whose intention had been frustrated by that sharp warning, did not drop the fork, but sank its points to the ground as he answered: "It's no use talking to me. There's been no ladies along here. Not since nine this morning. I'll swear to that.... You'll find the boss in his office, more like than not, if you go the other way. It's the green door. But you'll be a wise guy not to take that tone with him." He turned to go back into the room from which he had come, and then paused to say: "There's no call to blab that you've seen me. Mum's not a bad word." Perhaps he was not as dull as he had first looked.

Eustace tried the other passage. He supposed that the remaining seconds could not be many before the unceremonious manner of his entrance would have roused alarm and search. Already he might have expected to encounter more opposition in such a place than he had had to meet—would, indeed, have met a very different reception but for the manner of his entrance, and the dispositions which its proprietor had made to warn himself against approaching dangers of other sorts, and from other directions, a few minutes before.

He saw that his chance of finding Billie and bringing her safely out of those foul-smelling dens must depend upon swiftness first, and then upon bluff and threat, and would be slender at best. He made straight for the green-painted door, and thrust it open without the pause which a knock would mean.

It had been just as Maurice Beal had snapped his fingers to indicate the easy celerity of Billie's approaching end that his steps had sounded along the linoleum-covered passage, and Billie's eyes had lightened, for they were those which she knew and had been faintly hoping to hear.

"I think," she said, "that you have made one of the last mistakes that you ever will." She did not suppose that Eustace had come alone.

Her expression, even more than her words, drew her opponent's eyes, so that he was not instant to see who came in at the door, which he did not doubt to be one of his own men, and that second may have been no less to him than a vital loss.

He looked up to a levelled pistol, and to hear words that he did not like. "Put your hands up! And tell that beast to lie down. I can shoot more quickly than it can spring. And I'd rather kill you than not."

Maurice Beal raised his hands, but no more than a few inches, spreading them apart with a slight shrug, that it seemed a natural attitude for him to take. "You would be a fool," he said. "You would shoot me, and the Holy Virgin would have the lady you came to save."

"I have more shots than one. *Look at the beast*. I shall not warn you again."

The jaguar had half risen, its eyes moving balefully from Billie to this loud-voiced intruder at the open door. Had Eustace advanced, it is probable that it would have sprung at him at once, but, while he stood there, it waited uncertainly for its master's word.

Maurice Beal looked down at it, and said a few words in a foreign tongue, at which its tail moved. Its head sank on to its paws. But its eyes remained alert, suspicious. Its whole attitude showed that it was held back by no more than its master's will.

"You'd better come," Eustace said. "There's no use in prolonging this."

Billie rose, her eyes fixed upon, and endeavouring to subdue, those of the crouching beast. She said, without turning her eyes: "Eustace, let me have that pistol while you see whether Mr. Beal has got any arms. There's a hefty stick in the corner behind you. When I've got him covered you might secure that, too."

"You're sure you could use it?" he asked doubtfully.

"I used to shoot rats when I was younger than I am now. I don't see why I shouldn't manage one more. But while you're feeling him over I want to keep one eye on our little friend (as Mr. Beal calls her) on the floor. I think it will be all right if you avoid any sudden movement, and if Mr. Beal understands that if there's any excitement the first bullet will be for him."

Eustace did not fall in with these suggestions exactly as he received them. He stepped back to the corner first, and while still keeping their human enemy covered, felt behind him and secured the bludgeon. He transferred the revolver to Billie's lifted hand, and then, taking care to avoid any abrupt movement, such as might rouse the watchful jaguar to action too quick to check, shortened the knobbed stick in his left hand, while his right investigated Mr. Beal's apparel with a thoroughness which discovered not only a heavy loaded pistol, such as a man who spent his days among untamed beasts had some reason to carry, but a long sheath-knife also, suspended from a concealed belt, which was loaded also with what felt like small stones, and might be called diamonds at a first guess.

"You can keep that pistol," Eustace said. "We've got quite an arsenal now. We'd better back quietly to the door and transfer the key to the outside. But I must disconnect the telephone first."

"You don't think we'd better tie him up?"

"No. I think every second may count in getting out without further trouble, if it's not already too late. We must trust to a quick rush and the locked door behind us. And tying him up would be ticklish work with that beast looking on."

"Very well. But don't you think he'd better sit on it while we retire?"

It was obviously a sound idea. The scowling Maurice was ordered to leave his chair and seat himself on the jaguar's back, to discourage that animal from any abruptness of movement when she saw her master's enemies in the act of retreat.

Next moment they were outside the door, and had the satisfaction of turning a heavy key.

CHAPTER XIV.

The Spectacular Exit of Maurice Beal

SUPERINTENDENT BACKWASH'S dispositions had been thorough as well as swift.

Within twenty minutes of his receiving Eustace's call a cordon of local police had been cast in a wide circle around the vicinity of Adam Street, with instructions to close gradually upon the premises of Maurice Beal, and to detain anyone attempting to break the net whom they should recognize as being in his employment, in however humble a capacity.

By the time of his own arrival, with the armed squad on whom the duty of entering the building would fall, this cordon had been tightly drawn, with three incidental arrests, of an importance which could not be immediately determined. Beyond that, no one had been seen to enter or leave the premises. The shop in Adam Street stood empty. It might be significant that the strongly barred gates in Trevor Street had been closed, but a constable who worked that beat said that this would often occur during the daytime, presumably when no deliveries were expected or despatches being sent out.

It was only thirty-two minutes after Eustace's call had been received that Superintendent Backwash, accompanied by Inspectors Pearce and Baker, entered the shop. The bell clanged its usual warning, but no one came. Waiting no more than a few seconds, while they surveyed with professional curiosity the blood stains and broken glass that were distributed on the floor, they tried the inner door, and found it to be secured on the inside. Superintendent Backwash looked at it with curiosity. "Pearce," he said, "what do you think of this?"

"I think it's been forced open, sir. Not many hours ago."

"So do I. From this side."

That was the puzzling point. Someone had been breaking in, not out. What should be the meaning of that? The superintendent's thoughts went to Miss Wingrove, who had not been seen, and to her brother, about whose movements nothing was known since he had left the call-box in Whitechapel Road. Only a garbled account of how he had fought with a man there, and one or other of them had been knocked down, had come to the ears of the police.

Getting near to, though not reaching the truth, they looked at the damaged door, and imagined Eustace finding it locked and breaking it down in single-handed effort to effect his sister's rescue.

Now the door had been secured again from the inside. Not with the bolt that Eustace had shot. That had been damaged beyond quick repair when the door had been forced by the men he shut out. But some heavy articles had been wedged against it.

"It's no use losing time here," Superintendent Backwash said, as he hammered on it without response. "Call in a couple of men to burst it open. A crowbar ought to do it in half a minute. It isn't strong.... But what's that? You see to this, Pearce. And be careful when you get it open. You don't know what may be on the other side. Baker, you'd better come with me and see what's happening in Trevor Street."

From that direction police whistles shrilled. Coming out to the street they saw that the crowd in Whitechapel Road, now held back by a line of blue-uniformed constables, was in a state of swaying excitement. Some were trying to press toward Trevor Street, others to flee from it, as fear or curiosity proved the livelier urge. From the crowd beyond sight a woman screamed on a note which rose shrilly above the din. A word was passed from mouth to mouth, and the whole crowd broke and ran, leaving the blue line in an empty street.

As Superintendent Backwash came into the main thoroughfare a sergeant shouted an order. The line of constables, which had previously allowed passage on the further pavement of the Whitechapel Road now closed completely across it, drawing their batons as they did so.

"What is it, Mathews?" the superintendent asked. "Are they trying to break out?"

"No, sir. Not if I've heard right. Not exactly. They're turning loose the wild beasts. And I should say—well, sir, there's a smell."

He looked up. The idea had only to be mentioned to be accepted as a fact. Faint but unmistakable was the scent of fire. Already there was a darker film spreading beneath the heavy leaden gloom of the

London sky. And while they spoke there came the sound of a shot—and then of several.

"You'd better go round to Trevor Street at once, Baker, and see what your men are doing there. I'll be with you in three minutes." Saying this, the superintendent turned back to the Adam Street shop, to assure himself that any living creatures, men or beasts, which might attempt the use of that exit would be adequately received.

Being satisfied on this point, and seeing that the inner door of the shop was already in process of being battered in, he entered a police car which had been parked at the other side of the street, and drove round to Trevor Street.

The rumour that the wild animals had been loosed was at least premature, as he had more than half expected to find, and though the events that followed in the next hour were among the most bizarre in the history of London's criminality, or its famous fires, it might still be doubted how much was the deliberate action of a cornered and unscrupulous malefactor, how much was accident, and how much was the opportunism which takes swift advantage of that which it has not planned.

The origin of the fire was not, and can never now be, certainly determined. That it was the deliberate deed of a man who saw it to be the only method by which he could destroy the false-bottomed crates, and the stores of illicit drugs which were actually on his premises at the time, was a popular belief which there is no evidence to disprove. But is it not more probable that it was accidental in its beginning—perhaps from the smouldering of straw which had not been extinguished with sufficient care in the anaconda's cage—and that Maurice Beal, possibly reflecting upon his ample insurance of stock and premises, saw in it a means of destroying the evidences of his guilt, which he was in no haste to check?

Again, though it may be true that he liberated some ferocious beasts and some poisonous snakes, as well as the huge constrictor that its warehouses held, and though he may have expected that they would prepare the way for his safer flight, it may be doubted that he would have considered such a desperate expedient had it not been suggested to him by the natural impulse to free them from the blazing cages.

Men who spend their lives in handling, feeding, and often grooming wild animals in captivity lose much of the fears which are felt by those who are less initiated to what they are. Under the terror of fire, the wildest, the most ferocious animal, the most deadly snake, may lose all impulses either of hate or hunger in the panic of overmastering fear. It will crouch abjectly by the side of its natural foe or its natural prey.

As the smoke rolled down the passages, the order to open cages, the contents of which must otherwise have been suffocated or burned alive, with whatever motive it may have been given, did not seem to those who obeyed it to be an operation particularly dangerous to themselves.

Below, the police, looking up from a street which they had cleared of all civilian traffic, saw a reflection from the upper windows suggesting fire. The next moment a thin wisp of smoke drifted lazily from the roof. The order to call the fire stations had scarcely been obeyed when it had become a thick ruddy-centred column rising toward the sky.

Next moment the heavy gates were swung open, and a black panther ran out onto the pavement. It came a few paces forward, looking round with fierce but bewildered eyes, ran back, and then came out again as it smelled that which it dreaded more than a human foe. It is improbable that it would have done any harm. It might have been quite easy to corner and cage again had the operation been undertaken by experienced men. But a member of the detective squad who was inclined to boast of a skill in firearms which he had lacked opportunities of demonstrating to the approval of his superiors saw a chance here which they might praise and could scarcely blame. He fired, hitting the animal in the shoulder, and with the hot pain of that wound it became a raging devil, springing on its tormentor with tearing claws, and leaving him between life and death when, a moment later, half a dozen of his comrades' bullets—one of which found a mistaken home in his own leg—had brought it to a quick end.

Here again chance may have played its part in developing the climax of the event. The volley of shots, at a time when there had been no clash, or indeed contact of any kind, between the police and those who were still nominally law-abiding and law-protected citizens within, heard by men who were inwardly conscious not only of drug-smuggling activities but of (legally if not morally) more serious crimes which had been incidental thereto, may have been interpreted as showing that they were already surrounded by those who knew them for what they were, and would treat them according to their own merciless code....

Such was the position when Superintendent Backwash appeared on the scene. The first fire engine had not arrived. Every moment the smoke rose more densely above, and the upper windows showed more brightly. Those who could see through the open gateway observed some movements of men. Otherwise there was no sign of human life.

From the burning building there came such a clamour of strange and discordant cries as may not have been heard together by human ears since the ark grounded at Ararat and its menagerie scattered abroad.

"Inspector Baker," Superintendent Backwash said with the briskness which action brings, "take ten men into the building and arrest whoever you find within. Shoot if they resist. Any animals which do not appear dangerous should be released. And, of course, birds. I don't know what to say about tigers or snakes. We'll hope the firemen will be able to keep it under. Anyway, they should know what to do."

As he spoke, the loud bells of the first engines could be heard coming along the Whitechapel Road. Not waiting for them, Inspector Baker led his men forward to the burning building. He was detained a moment by Superintendent Backwash's voice: "Oh, and Miss Wingrove and Mr. Limbrook may be in there, though they're more likely to be on the other side, if they're alive. But don't fail to look out for them."

Inspector Baker was a brave man. One who would risk much for his own honour and more for that of the C.I.D. As he entered the gateway he was met by a snake, fawn-coloured and white, about three feet in length, with a very small flat head. It was slipping rapidly over the ground when it found its way barred by a file of advancing men. Its neck rose: its tongue flickered: it hissed defiance.

Inspector Baker did not give ground, though he had a great horror of snakes, and he made a sound guess that there would be death in a bite from that tiny sharp-toothed mouth. He drew his pistol and fired. The raised head was a small mark. It was little blame to him that he missed.

But, at the sound of the shot, the snake swerved. It slipped past the file of men, moving ever faster for a succession of bullets that pursued it but did not hit, and disappeared down a cellar grating.

Against that menace Inspector Baker's men had held their places, with his example to shame them from retreat; but as they went forward again, and were met by the huge bulk of an anaconda thirty-two feet in length, and advancing, in its terror of the fire from which it had broken free, at a pace which might not be easily matched by an active man, they broke and scattered, running wildly to right and left.

78

Inspector Baker stood his ground alone in the reptile's path. He poured out the contents of his automatic, and a peashooter would have done as much to check its advance. He jumped aside at the last moment, utterly disregarded by the fire-frightened monster, and, as he did so, Superintendent Backwash's chauffeur, to whom an almost equal tribute of admiration must be given, obeying the direction of his superior officer, drove his car at the anaconda's head.

The hot radiator must have struck it a smashing blow. The car lurched over its neck, with its two off wheels in the air. The superintendent, with an automatic in either hand, was firing out of the near window into its body. The car might have overturned, but the coils of the great snake swept round it, preventing that. Those who looked on heard the panels crack. Escaping petrol burst into flame.

It was only the presence of the firemen, and the fact that they got a hose to work upon it without a moment's delay, that saved the two men from a ghastly death. One door had jammed under the pressure of the snake's coils, but the other had cracked open, and through this they stumbled out, drenched with water, scorched with flame, and endangered by the blind threshing of the tortured reptile, as a volley of bullets tore into its burnt and damaged length.

It lay still at last, one coil, no longer aware of pain, roasting across the blaze of the burning car. But by this time it had become a mere incident of the pandemonium of the street. For it had not come out alone. Smaller snakes seemed everywhere underfoot. A pair of pumas, one dropping blood as it ran, were charging blindly through ranks of police who were afraid to fire lest it should be their comrades whom they would kill, and afraid, as they stepped, to take their eyes from the snake-infested ground. Other animals, some being of the larger carnivorous fauna of South America, and others of harmless habits but of queer fantastic forms, which were an almost equal terror to those who did not know their natures, swarmed into the street. Long-tailed monkeys festooned gutters and window-ledges, and scattered chattering over the roofs. A great condor, with a twelve-foot spread of dusky, moth-eaten wings, rising with difficulty into the air, clung flapping for some uncertain moments to a first-story window-ledge on the other side of the street, before daring to loose, and then, with sufficient air under its wings, soared out of sight in the smoky sky.

Among the chaos of fire and water, of escaping beast and reptile and bird, the firemen worked stolidly on, as their training impelled them to do, their feet protected the while by their high boots from the deadly danger of the smaller poisonous snakes that wriggled about the street.

Following the exodus of the beasts, a covered van came out of the gateway. It was an unfortunate moment for it, for a fresh fire-engine had just arrived, and its crew were in the act of attaching a hose, which they had been ordered to direct upon the angle of the building overlooking the gateway, to which, in the upper stories, the fire had begun to spread. A prompt order from Inspector Baker turned its nozzle upon the driver of the emerging van. Fortunately for its occupants, in the second before he was directly hit and swept ignominiously from his seat, the drenched driver had checked his speed and was backing into the yard. The van swerved into the side walk, giving its occupants no more than a rough jolt.

They tumbled out, Beal, with the Holy Virgin beside him, leading the way. They had been prepared for bullets, and were themselves bristling with arms. It had seemed a possible plan to shoot their way through the distracted ranks of the police, and then abandon the van and scatter among the crowds. But they had been met with an element which they could not face.

"Close the gates," Maurice Beal ordered. "We must try Adam Street." Perhaps, he thought, there might be nothing worse than staves or bullets to face in the other street. They must try to fight their way out on foot through the shop door.

But could they get back to those premises? The doubt caused him to look up at the wooden bridge, which, two stories high, was directly above his head.

He saw that it was blazing fiercely at the nearer end. It would be a desperate—an impossible way. Yet, as he looked, there were those who attempted to cross.... And the next moment it fell.

He turned to jump from beneath the falling wreckage. He stumbled over the Holy Virgin, who, divided between terror of surrounding fire and loyalty to him who had been her master from earliest memories, had crouched, whining, beside his feet...

The gates had not been closed. The fire hose, playing on those who would have run forward, had prevented that. Inspector Baker, with a dozen men, had rushed into the yard behind its barrage. He saw Maurice Beal lying face downward, with the main joist of the bridge on his broken back.

Whimpering with terror, snarling at a smouldering plank, the jaguar crouched beside him. A man who was accustomed to feed her interposed as a policeman was about to fire, and threw a sack over the yellow head.

THE RETURN OF THE MILDEW GANG, BY S. FOWLER WRIGHT

Their leader being dead, the men surrendered their arms without difficulty. What had they done but obey orders? Why were they armed but to protect themselves from the savage beasts which they had been directed to set free to save them from the advancing fire? If there were anything wrong, it must be the fault of a dead man.... There was one who, being sharply questioned, volunteered to show the secret hiding place, behind a serpent's cage which was yet unburned, where the drugs were stored until they could be safely removed.

CHAPTER XV.

A Problem of Going Down

EUSTACE and Billie had stood in a moment of hesitation outside Maurice Beal's door A sense of exaltation at their triumph over him was natural, and with it, in Billie's heart, one of immeasurable relief from a deadly peril so nearly missed. She had looked over the very edge of the pit of death, and her breath was short at the memory of what she had just endured.

But with exaltation there must be anxiety also: the game was half won, but no more. They looked backward and forward along the passage, asking themselves which way they should go. It came to Eustace's mind that there must be another way out, in another street, and that they might have a better prospect of peaceful exit by finding that than by returning the way of violence which he had come.

"Shall we try this way?" he asked.

"Shall we?" She was doubtful. "There is another long passage round there, and stairs, and dens. There is one you go through—I suppose that can't be necessary—with an enormous snake. It's not a quick way out. I suppose you came over the bridge?"

"Yes."

"Then let's try that."

"Very well. Anything's better than wasting time."

That sounded sense. But, in fact, it made little difference. They had disconnected his public telephone, but had failed to observe the private instrument by which Maurice Beal communicated with other parts of the premises. Even while they spoke, he had given orders which barred all exits, unless they should fight their way past those who were more numerous than themselves, more ruthless, and more expert in the use of arms.

With the loaded weapons in their hands, they had some hope that there would be none with courage to bar their way. But they did not anticipate that the first bullet would be fired, not by them, but by a man whom they did not see

So, however, it was. Billie was the first to step on to the bridge. As she did so, she was covered by a man who looked out of an attic window on the opposite side, with a heavy sporting rifle directed upon the door out of which she came. Had the event occurred in his native country, she would have been a dead woman, for he was not one who would miss at twelve-yards' range. But he was a cautious man, who remembered that promiscuous homicide is discouraged by English law. He thought he obeyed orders sufficiently nearly when he directed his first discharge at the rail of the bridge, from which splinters flew. Not waiting for a second, Eustace pulled her back.

"It looks," he said, "as though we might do better the other way."

"I don't know," she answered doubtfully, feeling a strong disinclination to be shot at again.

"I suppose the police will soon be here."

"Superintendent Backwash said he wouldn't do anything."

"*Said he wouldn't*—there must be something wrong about that."

"He made it quite clear. Emphatic, you might say. He said we'd no business to be here, and must get out of our own troubles our own way."

"I can't believe he said that."

"Well, not exactly. He implied that I was making much out of nothing, and that I'd better go quietly home, and should find you there."

"You gave him the address?"

"Yes. I made that clear."

"Then it's only a question of time. We want a quiet corner till then."

Eustace was inclined to agree, though the memory of Superintendent Backwash's voice rankled in his mind. Anyway, it was a poor game wandering in a building they did not know, to encounter those who would shoot on sight.

They found a stair which mounted to the third story, up which they went. They came to a thick oak door, the upper part of which was set with iron bars through which they could see a long passage. It all seemed silent, lifeless, probably only used when there should be an exceptionally heavy stock overflowing the accommodation below.

"We ought," Eustace said, "to be able to find somewhere along here where we shouldn't be easy to reach." He turned an iron handle—there was no appearance of any lock—and the door opened. As it swung behind them they were disconcerted, for a moment, to see that there was no handle on the inside. But that was a trouble which could wait. They went on, trying locked doors which roused no response, until they came to a room the door of which had been broken down.

It was empty, except for a few wisps of scattered straw, and had a queer repellent smell. At one place there was a wide stain, suggesting blood. In the wall of the passage opposite the door there was a water tap with a length of hose coiled beside it. Billie turned the tap, and had the satisfaction of seeing it run. "We shan't die of thirst," she said with satisfaction. Eustace said nothing in reply. He had a more disconcerting vision in which they ran for the vital water while bullets sang down the passage from the iron-barred door. Neither of them had any foresight of the use to which that tap would be put in the next hour.

"I wonder what happened here last," Billie said, gazing at that dark stain on the floor.

"Perhaps it's just as well that you don't know. But certain that no one could come upon us without being overheard."

There was satisfaction in that, which may not have been lessened when they looked through a window crusted with dirt, and observed that they were opposite the attic from which the shot had come which had driven them back. The man was still at the window. He did not see them. He was looking down, where the muzzle of his rifle pointed. It would be easy to keep out of his observation. They stepped aside.

They talked for a few minutes, relating their experiences since they had parted so short a time before.

After that, minutes became hours, while they stood in that bare place with its evil smell.

"I wonder," Eustace said, "how long we're going to endure this."

"I could stand it; but there's a smell of fire that I don't like."

"I'm trying not to smell anything."

"It's no use taking it like that. There's something on fire somewhere. It's getting worse."

"It's your burnt dress."

"It's more than that. But there's an idea there. Suppose the straw wasn't really put out?"

"Do you think that possible?"

"No. I think it was. But there's a fire somewhere." Eustace did not dispute that. He had spoken from the first to reassure her, rather than from his own conviction. The smell was becoming stronger every moment. Looking obliquely through the window, he saw a darker shadow than came from its own grime or the leaden sky.

He stepped boldly up to the glass. "The man's gone from the other side. I believe the building's on fire."

"Then we'd better have another try to get over the bridge, before it's too late."

"It may be even more risky to try too soon."

They paused in doubt between the terror of fire and of human foes.

"We'd better go back on to the landing, anyway," she said, "and have a look round."

"I'll go first, while you wait here."

"What's the sense in that?"

"If we got halfway along the passage, and anyone shot at us through the bars, there'd be nowhere to take cover at all. There's no sense in both risking that, when one would do."

"If they should, there'd be a better chance for us if two could shoot back. I think we'll both go. But I don't believe anyone will be there.... How shall we open the door?"

"We must blow it open if necessary. A couple of shots ought to do that."

It might not have proved so simple, but it was not tried. When they looked through the iron bars it was into a passage which was filled with smoke. It rolled up from the stairs, which burned fiercely.

"We couldn't get down there; and it's probably worse below."

Eustace answered with that which had been in his mind before. "If that attic's opposite, the bridge must be just below the window of the room where we were."

"What help is there in that?"

"We could knock the window out and jump down." She heard this dubiously. It was a most unattractive idea, but Eustace was already running back. Years ago he had seen an old building burn, and he knew how great their danger might be. Fortunately the floor of the passage was concreted, as were some of the rooms.

As he came to the tap he turned it on. Seeing that the water would pass away through a drain beneath it, he attached the hose, letting the water pour out along the passage. It must do some good, though it might not be much.

The window was small and had been nailed up. To give them space to climb out, it was clear that the frame must go. Thankful for Maurice Beal's sharp knife, Eustace worked desperately, smashing away heavy bludgeon, and twice with a bullet's help.

Billie watched with no enthusiasm. Would no one come? Firemen? Police? Even repentant dealers in unfamiliar beasts? She would have seen the work take longer to do. She was sure that she was not going out there.

But by now smoke was drifting along the passage. As the window gave way the draught drew it with a quickly increasing density into the room.

Eustace looked out. "Yes," he said, "the bridge is just underneath. This window's over the door. It's not a long drop. But it's on fire at this end. Bring the hose, will you?"

The hose was fortunately long enough, though only just. It could not be fixed so that it would pour downward. It must be held. But, directed thus, the water hissed on the burning wood. After a minute of this the fire was driven back. The surface of the planks became wet and black. But their undersides would still be burning. Every moment they must become less secure.

Eustace wondered, if this end were burnt through, would the bridge be sustained from the further side? He thought not. When he had passed over it, it had looked rotten enough to fall without the assistance of fire.

He withdrew the hose. "You'd better go first," he said. "I can let you down till your feet almost touch the planks."

She looked out. "I can't do that, Eustace. I really won't. It's all fire."

It was true that, as the water had been withdrawn, the flames from beneath the planking, fed from the burning door, had burst upward again. But as she drew her head back she coughed in the acrid smoke that was now pouring thickly past them through the window gap.

"You've got to," he said, "and quickly. It won't get better. It will get worse. If you're quick there's no danger at all."

As he said it he asked himself, "Was it true?" For all he knew, the whole bridge might give way when she descended upon it, or the planks, half burnt through, might break under her feet. Yet he must send her first, for she was the lighter weight, and he could lower her so that she would strike those rotten, half-burnt planks with the minimum of shock. She might pass in safety where his greater weight would break it through. And, after what she had said, he was less than sure that, if he should go first, she would follow at all. For every reason she must go first.

While he spoke he had picked up the hose, which had been spilling water around their feet, and directed it on to the bridge again.

"I'll soak it till the last moment," he said, "so be ready the instant I draw it in."

"It's no good, Eustace. My dress would catch. I should burn to death."

"It won't if we soak it first. You'll burn to death if you stay here."

Her voice changed. "Of course, I'll try, if it's really necessary. I'm not really a coward."

"I know that. You're a very brave girl."

He drew in the hose and turned it upon her dress. Neither of them was of a demonstrative nature, but they kissed as he helped her to slip over the sill. It might be for the last time.

Next moment she was suspended by his hands only, hanging over the bridge.

"Eustace, it's burning me. I really can't. It's too hot."

"Nonsense. I'm loosing now. It's the only way."

There was not more than a few inches to drop. She felt the burning planks giving way under her feet. She turned in the choking heat and ran quickly across. She could only guess how badly her feet were burned. She saw the spreading singe on her sleeve, and pressed out the fire with a scorched hand.... Why did not Eustace come?

She looked back into the smoke, which had become too dense for anything to be clearly seen. He was using the hose again. Now he was climbing out. He hung by his hands from the sill. He had a drop of almost two feet. As he struck the other end of the bridge, it cracked and jarred, making her conscious that she still stood on its structure, though she was within a few inches of the jamb of the door. Fortunately for both of them, she stepped back, clearing his way.

In another moment he was across, and at the same instant the bridge fell completely. The weight of his descent upon it had severed the burning end, and it had not been built to maintain itself from a single side. Had she stood where she would have obstructed his leaping clear, that last second had been one too late.

He had been burnt more severely than she. It was the last day for a week that he would be able to walk abroad. But what was that to those whose lives had been won from the perils of the last hour?

They stood defenceless to those who surrounded them in the next minute, but it was the voice of Inspector Parker which said: "Miss Wingrove, I am glad to see you are safe. There's no fire on this side yet, and we're hoping to hold it back, but you'd better come down while you can."

CHAPTER XVI.

The Attitude of Inspector Cauldron

INSPECTOR CAULDRON had had no reason to be dissatisfied with himself or with the course of events, either in connection with the Houghton homicide—the first important case which (owing to the sudden illness of a superior officer) had been placed in his hands—or the partial exposure of the activities of the Mildew Gang which had, by a singular circumstance, resulted therefrom. In fact, he had won praise.

And, beyond that, there had been the possibility that if Mr. James Catsgill should recover from the effects of the murderous "accident" of which he had been the victim, he might make disclosures which would supplement the legally insufficient evidences already in the hands of the C.I.D. sufficiently to justify the arrest of Cornelius Mildew, which would be likely to bring fresh honour to the officer who had the investigation in hand.

It is true that the telegram which had been sent to Scotland Yard at Miss Brell's suggestion had caused some disquiet, especially to Superintendent Backwash, who had been primarily responsible for the sending of Mr. Limbrook and his sister to Scotland, and for the publicity of their exodus thereto. It had become evident—unless the telegram were an improbable hoax—that this procedure had neither led Mildew to regard them as negligible, nor removed them beyond the radius of his power; and that it was genuine—even though its sender could not be traced—had approximated to certainty when the accuracy of the information it contained had been established, a man giving the name of Bolton having lodged a damaged car at the garage which had been recommended to the attention of the police.

But the blunder, if such it were, and whatever unpleasant consequence it might have had, or still threaten, for those immediately concerned, was not one for which he had any responsibility. His own part in the matter had gone no further than to carry out the instructions he received, which he had competently done.

Yet Eustace's telegram had perturbed him beyond logical cause. The fact was he could not regard the matter with the abstract equanimity normal to the official mind. His contacts with Billie Wingrove had been of too personal a character. She might remember him with indignation as one who (in a moment of hastened action) had laid soiled shoes on a chiffon dress; but, while he thought nothing of that (being indeed, utterly unconscious of his offence), he had other memories, such as are not required to be retained in a detective-inspector's mind. He had endeavoured to discourage them, under the mistaken presumption (most discreditable to his acumen as a member of the C.I.D.) that she was the fiancée of Eustace Limbrook, and only learned the truth as they were flying away over the Midland counties.

Superintendent Backwash, handling the telegram as though it met his hand with a nettle's sting, on the afternoon following its delivery, by which time its authenticity was beyond reasonable doubt, had said irritably: "It was all Tolbooth's fault from the first. He suggested the Scotland plan. I don't suppose it would have entered my head."

Inspector Cauldron had remained discreetly silent. It was no part of his duty to allocate responsibility among his superior officers, and they both knew that Chief Inspector Tolbooth had no official connection with the case. A conversational suggestion from him was for the superintendent to take or leave, and, if he took it, the responsibility became his either for praise or blame.

As though conscious of the weakness of his complaint, Superintendent Backwash went on: "And Tolbooth knew all the time? He knew she was Limbrook's sister? I don't suppose I should ever have adopted the idea if I hadn't thought they'd get married there. That was the whole point of the plan."

The inspector saw that, as a matter of equity, if not of official etiquette, there was substance in this contention. People who have gone off to Scotland to get married are hardly likely to be actively concerned in aiding the police in London to run down a drug-smuggling gang. It would not merely have demonstrated that the police did not require them to remain in town; it would have given explanation of why they went.

An exact justice would also have observed that Chief Inspector Tolbooth had not been made aware of this aspect of the superintendent's plan.

Inspector Cauldron, still maintaining discretion, said no more than that most of them had been misled about that.

"But the question is," the superintendent had gone on, recovering his own discreetness of speech as it met his auditor's receptive passivity, "what we are to do now. They seem to have given Mildew's jackals the slip, after—I should call it about ten to one—being responsible for ditching the car. And, when they'd done that, they must have moved fast. The time and place where Limbrook put in that wire are proofs of that. And they must have done it by road. That ought to be enough to put us on the right track."

"They'll be avoiding Mildew, and probably given up relying on us. They won't be easy to follow."

"Oh, they hadn't given up having help from us! They give us our job putting salt on this Bolton's tail. They want to rely on us and themselves too. They're a lively pair.... All the same, we ought to run them down before Mildew can. He may be a clever man, but he hasn't got our resources, and he hasn't got this telegram to start him smelling on the right track."

"You'd like me to find them, whatever cost or trouble it means?"

"Yes. It's a thing that's got to be cleared up. And after what's happened Mildew will stick at nothing to run them down, and to finish them if he gets the chance. He may be a cool hand, but I'd bet there are few men today who are more frightened than he. We've got to find them, and find them first, or it'll be a bad day for them, and a nasty setback for us."

Inspector Cauldron, having got exactly what he wanted without asking for it, which is the clearest triumph of diplomacy, had gone, without further words, to execute the order he had received.

CHAPTER XVII.

MISS BRELL DISLIKES THE POLICE

WHEN Inspector Cauldron went to implement Superintendent Backwash's order that Mr. Limbrook and his sister were to be traced with the utmost celerity and at any cost, he had resolved to interpret this instruction in the most liberal spirit. If they were not traced and found within forty-eight hours, it would only be because the entire police force of the country, whipped up to its utmost vigilance, had proved unequal to so simple a task.

He did not, therefore, set out himself to make enquiries and discover elusive clues, being trained to a better method. He remained at the centre of the investigation to receive reports and direct subsequent movements.

There were two points from which such enquiries could originate—the garage where Bolton had deposited his damaged car, and the post office where Eustace's telegram had been handed in. The first of these supplied suggestive particulars of Miss Gloria Brell's association with the event; and enquiries at Brell Castle, and then at Brooklands, established a probability, if no more, that it was that lady's car which had conveyed those whom he sought to trace from the scene of the accident.

It was at least certain that Miss Brell had travelled south at a high speed, and the time and place from which Mr. Limbrook had sent the telegram were consistent with his having been in the lady's car.

To seek an interview with Miss Brell became the obvious course, and, in view of the fact that she was entered for a race on the next day, it appeared likely to be a simple operation.

But Miss Brell was a lady of many and rapid movements. She might be racing at Brooklands tomorrow, but that had not prevented her visiting Southampton today, where a friend was to be met. She could probably be reached on the telephone, Inspector Cauldron was told by the janitor of her Brook Street flat, at the Royal Hotel there.

So he found it to be; but there was little satisfaction in the conversation that followed. Before he could get further than a statement of who he was, he was interrupted by a curt, "Well, you can leave it at Brook Street, can't you? There's no reason to ring me up here."

"Leave what?" he queried in some natural uncertainty of the lady's meaning.

"The summons, of course."

"It's not a matter of a summons. I want to know where you put down the two passengers you brought from Scotland, and any information you can give me as to where they may be now."

"Put down who? I haven't said I picked anyone up yet."

"No. But we have no doubt that you did."

"I don't suppose you know anything of the kind."

"I don't think, Miss Brell, if you'll excuse me saying it, you're taking quite the right tone. It's the duty of every member of the public to give us any assistance they can in the difficult enquiries we sometimes have to make, and, in this case, it is in the interest of the people themselves."

"How'm I to know that? I know how quick you always are to assist me! Now look here, Inspector, you say it's my duty to tell you something you don't know. Well, I'll do that. You just hang on for three minutes and I'll add up all the fines I've paid in the past year. When you've got that figure you'll know just how I feel about giving you a leg up, even if it were anything I were able to do."

"I'm sorry you take it like that, Miss Brell. We want to trace these people so that we may give them protection they may need very seriously. If anything should happen to them owing to your attitude, you might be subject to very serious censure."

There was a moment's silence after this, the significance of which was not easy to guess. The inspector's argument might have reduced Miss Brell's defiant attitude to one of doubt, or she might be engaged in the arithmetical exercise which she had proposed. But when she spoke at last it was to say no more than: "It seems to me that you're assuming a whole lot that you don't know. But I shall be in London tomorrow, and you can see me then if you think it's worthwhile. I don't promise I shall tell you anything. I don't say that I've got anything to tell."

"Where can I see you then?"

"Brooklands, after the race. Not before. I'm not going to be bothered before that."

"But if I met your car? I shouldn't keep you ten minutes."

"I shan't come up by car. I'm not a fool. I shall come by train."

"Then if I were at Waterloo at the...."

"If you pester me there, you won't get a word. Not then or later. I wish you policemen could understand that people sometimes say what they mean."

Miss Brell rang off. Inspector Cauldron reluctantly recognized that he had met a woman against whom his utmost pertinacity would not avail. The time and place must be her selection, or he would get nothing at all. But he had the satisfaction of feeling that he was on the right track. Had she known nothing, she would certainly have replied in a different way.

So he said to Superintendent Backwash when he reported this telephone skirmish to him.

"A bit raw with us over her speed limit fines," the superintendent commented philosophically. "You can't blame her for that. The trouble is that some people's driving's safer at sixty miles an hour than that of others at twenty-five, and we're not allowed to make any discrimination. I don't know that Miss Brell ever did as much harm as laming a dog, but I believe she holds the record for making unwilling contributions to public funds.... All the same, she was stalling now, for more reasons than that. She'll probably get in touch with Limbrook before you see her tomorrow. It means they're in London now, more likely than not. I wonder what sort of a hell of a mess they'll get us into before they've done."

The two officers had looked gloomily at each other, sharing an emotion that the superintendent felt more acutely in a professional—and the inspector in a more personal—way.

If Eustace Limbrook and his sister had come back to challenge the ruthless methods of the Mildew Gang, without even such protection as the police were able to give, their lives were of a very slight insurable value, and the manner of their decease might be such as the police, if they cannot avert, are expected to be able to solve, with evil consequences for those by whom it has been contrived; and the publicity of such a solution might involve exposure of much which would be of dubious credit to them.

"I ought," Inspector Cauldron replied, with a degree of self-condemnation which the occasion scarcely required, "to have got round that Brell woman to tell the tale a bit quicker than she'll do now. I'd say shooting's better than I deserve if Mildew gets on their track first and any harm happens to her."

Superintendent Backwash heard this bitter ejaculation with more surprise than it was his habit to show. He felt that the blame would be on his head rather than that of his subordinate officer if there should be tragedy to explain, and he had not expected such fervour on his account. Also, he noticed the somewhat confusing use of the final feminine pronoun, and, though he was far from wishing ill to Billie Wingrove, it was mishap to her brother which would be the more likely to lead to questions in the coroner's court, or the public Press, such as could not be turned aside without revelations the C.I.D. would wish to avoid.

"After what we'd done for him," he said, "he might at least have let us know his address."

"They might say that they'd taken our advice once about going away, and hadn't found it any too good."

The superintendent had reacted sharply to this irritating truth: "It was sounder advice, anyway, to tell them to clear off than to come back, and they'd be a lot safer if they'd let us know where they are now, I suppose you'll admit that."

It was a proposition that Inspector Cauldron had no wish to dispute, desiring nothing more than to trace these difficult and elusive allies. Besides that, he understood the superintendent's exasperation. Having resigned themselves to the policy of a continued period of watch-and-wait in regard to the head or heads of the Mildew Gang, it would bring no pleasure, and might he a source of grave embarrassment to the C.I.D., if that period of reluctant patience should be punctuated by the murders of those who had given them information which, differently handled, might have been of a decisive character; and of whom one had been before public notice during the past month as the victim of a police error to which it would be most unfortunate that attention should be directed again.

He said no more than that he thought Miss Brell could tell a lot if she would, and that she wouldn't find it easy to get rid of him till she'd been persuaded to spit it out. But he must wait, with whatever impatience, till tomorrow for that to occur.

So he did; and he was just starting out for this projected interview when he was diverted by the superintendent's announcement that the missing pair had come on to the scene again in no different manner, and received instructions to proceed to the arrest of Cornelius Mildew.

He would have preferred to have been allocated to the raiding of Mr. Beal's menagerie, and the rescue of an imperilled girl, but, from the aspect of his profession, it was better to be the principal in what was likely to be the most important, as it would certainly be one of the most startling, arrests of recent years, rather than one of several subordinate officers in a raid of which Superintendent Backwash would take control. Nor could he have any doubt that the raiding operations would be conducted with speed and energy, and with every possible regard for the safety of those who had discovered, and been the first to enter, the place. It was true that Superintendent Backwash's verbal response to Eustace Limbrook's appeal had not been of a sympathetic or informative character, and how far his words may have been influenced by the irritation he had been feeling about the way in which the police had been kept in ignorance of the movements of the two amateur investigators is a problem of psychology which defies solution—he would have said, with sincerity, not in the smallest degree, but, on such a point, the roots of decision are not easy to reach—yet his sufficient motives in refusing to promise support had been that it would incline Mr. Limbrook to instant action, the urgency of which the superintendent did not minimize in his own mind, and that, if he should fall into the hands of those ruthless criminals before rescue could arrive, he could not reveal that which he did not know.

So Inspector Cauldron, his mind too fully occupied with the duty which had been entrusted to him to have leisure for wandering thoughts, set out to secure the arrest of a man who, he hoped, might yet be taken by surprise while in the imagined security of reputation and wealth, and innocent of criminal record or even associations, except through the gang which he controlled with such calculated aloofness that even those who were most influential in its operations might not have heard his name.

CHAPTER XVIII.

MR. MILDEW IS NOT AT HOME

INSPECTOR CAULDRON thought quickly, as the occasion required. The morning was advanced. Mildew might still be found at his dignified residence in Palace Gardens, or he might have driven into the city, as he sometimes would in the earlier hours of the day. In the afternoon he could usually be found at his club, where he would win or lose sums trivial to him at a respectable, competent, unadventurous game.

The club was the place where he could be most certainly and quietly arrested. He could be surprised there without previous warning. It was the place where he could be found most surely at the right hour. But it involved some delay, and any minute now might bring alarm to a man whose plans for such an emergency would almost certainly be of his customary efficiency.

The city was where, at this time, he would be most likely to be, but that is a vague address, and his places of call were many. He was known to lunch at many restaurants, seldom twice at one in the same week. Doubtless, one or more of these were points of contact with subordinate criminals, but this promiscuous habit made it harder to locate suspicion. The club, where he went regularly, was the one place where it would be certain that no illicit transaction would occur.

On the whole, Inspector Cauldron decided that Palace Gardens would be his best chance. He would go there himself, and alone. He did not think that Mildew would be foolish enough to resist arrest. His more probable attitude would be indignant repudiation of any criminal activities or associations, which, even now, might not be easy to prove. But, five minutes later, half a dozen capable subordinates would be on the scene. For there would not only be Mildew's removal to arrange. There would be the servants, who must be re-

97

garded dubiously, but against whom no charge could be made, to watch, and, if necessary, restrain from interference with the contents of the house. There would be a most thorough search to be made, for it; was upon the discovery of incriminating documents or other evidences that the success of the proceedings must largely depend.

Inspector Cauldron did not rely solely upon his own efforts. The matter was too important and too urgent for that. In ten minutes he had scattered a dozen capable officers in search of the wanted man, to arrest him wherever he might be found. He had detailed men to watch the club doors. He set off himself for Palace Gardens in a car that traffic regulations would not retard. He had little fear that Mildew would avoid a net so swiftly and widely cast....

The footman who opened the door had an appearance of dull respectability which might have daunted a less experienced or intelligent officer. He said, with polite disinterest, that Mr. Mildew was not at home. There was nothing in this to arouse suspicion. At that hour it might be most commonly true. There would be little wisdom in alarming the household staff while their master was still at large.

Inspector Cauldron asked, in his most casual voice: "Can you tell me how long he's likely to be?"

The footman was afraid that he could not say.

"I suppose you don't expect him before lunch?"

"If you will wait a moment, I will enquire."

Inspector Cauldron was offered a chair in the hall.

With no more than a moment's delay a butler appeared. His aspect was of the sobriety and discretion natural to his estate. He asked Inspector Cauldron's name. He read the card with an expressionless face. "You wish to see Mr. Mildew?" he enquired politely. "I could make an appointment for you for next Tuesday evening, or, subject to Mr. Mildew's confirmation, any time during the following day."

"I'm afraid I must see him before that."

Inspector Cauldron's voice had some curtness now. Was he being politely fooled? But the butler showed no consciousness of the change. Observing the proprieties of his own office, his attitude was indifferent to the lapses of other men.

"I'm afraid that would not be possible to arrange. I am not aware of Mr. Mildew's present address."

"You mean he's gone away and left none?"

"Yes, sir. That is the case."

"I suppose he doesn't often do that?"

"Very frequently, sir."

"And how about forwarding his letters under such circumstances?"

"Mr. Mildew's correspondence will await his return."

Inspector Cauldron saw that a decision must be instantly made, and that its responsibility must be entirely his. He had no search warrant. To invade the house of Cornelius Mildew in its master's absence, unless it should be justified by its results, would be a legal offence for which his superiors would have no scruple in leaving the blame to fall on his own shoulders, to which it would, indeed, rightly belong. He knew that Superintendent Backwash was risking as much, or more, in his Adam Street raid, of the result of which he was not yet aware; but so far, he had himself done no more than attempt to carry out the orders he had received. He could not have been blamed for that, even though he had arrested Mildew, and it had proved to be an indefensible error.

Now Cornelius Mildew might have gone away without any special cause for alarm having entered his mind. He might be intending to return on Tuesday, as he had said. But that was less than sure. Even though such absences might be frequent, and even though—which was much less certain—this might be one of the usual kind, he might read such news in the daily press as would cause him to change his plans. At the moment of indecision, as his mind balanced doubt, there came to him the memory of how Mr. Catsgill had said that their chance had been to risk arresting Mildew before any apprehension of such an event should have entered that gentleman's fertile and wary mind. Had they done it then, it was almost certain that they could have obtained evidence which would have justified it subsequently, and Catsgill would not be lying in hospital now, hovering on the edge of death, nor would Miss Wingrove have had occasion to face a peril from which he could only hope that she was being rescued safely. A risk which Superintendent Backwash elected to take should not be too much for him. He said firmly: "I have an urgent reason for seeing Mr. Mildew at once. I must ask you, in the name of the law, to give me any information you can which will enable me to find him."

He thought that the butler's eyes blinked at this, but, if so, it was an action so slight, so momentary, that it left him unsure, as the man replied with respectful imperturbability: "I am sorry, sir; but I can tell you no more than I have already done. It is not Mr. Mildew's custom to confide his movements to his domestic staff."

It was possible to imagine a faint note of most respectful rebuke in these harmless words, as though attention were delicately directed to the fact that inspectors of the C.I.D. cannot be expected to be familiar with the habits of gentlemen of Mr. Mildew's degree. It was possible, also, as Inspector Cauldron was quick to see, to interpret them as an assertion of innocence before accusation had raised its head. The man would have it clear that he was butler in that house and nothing other than that. He was in no way conversant with his master's private affairs. But, however they might be construed, they might still be literally true.

"In that case," he said, "I must take the liberty of searching the house."

The man looked a proper surprise. "I can assure you," he said, "that Mr. Mildew is not here."

"No, I had taken your word for that. It is Mr. Mildew's absence which will oblige me to search the house."

"It is a course of action," the man said, with a firmness equal to his own, "to which you will not expect me to give you any form of assent. I must protest against it most emphatically on Mr. Mildew's behalf. But I shall do nothing to obstruct you if you can satisfy me that you have legal warrant for what you do."

Inspector Cauldron saw that the butler, whether of good character or bad, was a discreet and capable man. His attitude was beyond reproach, and would yet leave the police—which meant himself alone—to bear the maximum of responsibility if they should be casting a net which would be empty when it should be drawn in. He could not even reply that legal warrant was his, as he should have been able to do. He answered boldly: "If you have any doubt of my authority, you can phone Chief Inspector Tolbooth at Scotland Yard."

Even the result of that enquiry would be less than sure. The answer would depend upon how much Tolbooth had heard of the day's events, and how much personal responsibility that particularly astute police officer would be prepared to take. But the risk had to be run, for it was certain that Superintendent Backwash would not be in. Probably, Cauldron thought, he would be asked to go to the instrument himself to explain what he was proposing to do. Well, there would be some satisfaction—probably some division of responsibility—in that. Even if he should be called off he could not be greatly blamed, one way or other.

But the test was not made. As he spoke his assistants were at the door. Their advent, following his own confident words, appeared to remove any doubt the butler might have had (which may not have been much) of the authority with which Inspector Cauldron was armed. He satisfied himself by repeating his protest in the hearing of the newcomers. He led the way through the house, as he was directed to do.

The domestic staff, being gathered into the kitchen in a half-frightened, half-curious group, proved to be of moderate numbers for so large a house, and of apparent respectability. The housekeeper, a quiet-mannered, elderly woman, said that she was also the cook. There were three subordinate female servants, of the usual designations, of whom two were present, and one was having her day out. There were the butler and footman. For a bachelor establishment of its kind it had an aspect of propriety, affluent but restrained. If the king of drug smugglers had any riotous vices they were not allowed to disturb the serenity of his own dignified residence. But it was mere justice—mere accuracy—to observe that his reputation was not of that kind.

Inspector Cauldron acted with thoroughness. He could not examine the contents of such a residence, in which any illicit correspondence or records were not likely to be obtrusively kept, in an hour or even a day. What he could he did, with no result that was satisfactory to him. Beyond that, he sealed desks and doors. He placed guards. He left orders with officers he could trust to arrest Mildew, if he should unexpectedly return. Incoming correspondence was to be impounded. The telephone was not to be used by the household staff, and if they should leave the house they were to be followed and their movements observed.

Had they all started off in different directions even the efficient officers he left in charge might have found this instruction difficult to carry out, consistently with the other duties they had undertaken. But, in fact, there was no such attempt. The servants remained at their posts, quietly and politely continuing their ordinary duties, so far as was possible under the police restrictions imposed upon them. In fact, they remained examples of law-abiding propriety. Acts of dubious legality were committed only by the police, and the conscience of Inspector Cauldron might, by the aspects of those around him, be the only one that was not entirely at rest.

But, he told himself, he had gone too far to consider the possibility of successful retreat. His only hope was that either his own investigations, or the raid which Superintendent Backwash was doubtless directing by this time in Adam Street, would obtain such evidence as would be their joint justification—and he saw, too clearly for his own comfort, that the one did not necessarily imply the other. The discovery of illegal practices in Whitechapel might leave the name of Mildew without a stain. But he had better hopes: and the counsels of prudence and inclination were united in urging that he would only increase his danger if he should allow himself to be retarded by scruples now.

CHAPTER XIX.

CONSTABLE HITCHINS HAS OPEN EYES

SUPERINTENDENT BACKWASH felt that he had good reason to be content. He had just satisfied the clamorous demands of the late evening Press, and promised that there should be more copy for the morning editions. It would be pleasant copy for him to read. The efficiency of the C.I.D. had uncovered one of the worst and most ingenious cases of drug smuggling in the history of that most infamous traffic, and the scoundrels concerned had set their own premises on fire in a vain effort to destroy the evidences of their guilt.

The spectacular circumstances of the fire would give the event an enormous publicity, and the name of Superintendent Backwash would be on every page. What could be better than that?

But Inspector Cauldron entered, and he had the look of a less satisfied man.

"No luck," he said laconically. "Mildew left this morning, and won't be back, so they say, till next Tuesday."

"If ever. Left no address, of course?"

"No. But there appears to be nothing in that. The servants say he often goes away for a weekend or longer and doesn't say where."

"That sounds likely enough. What do they do with his letters?"

"Just let them accumulate till he returns.... I've sealed everything up and left half a dozen men in charge. I've left nothing to chance. But I don't suppose there's anything incriminating where we shall find it."

Superintendent Backwash was, of course, inclined to take the more cheerful view.

"Anyway," he said, adopting responsibility for what was now going on at Palace Gardens more readily that Inspector Cauldron had expected him to do, "you've done the right thing. It's too late for half-measures now.

"If we push this hard, we ought to get all the evidence we require, even if Mildew's papers don't help us—and that's hard to believe, seeing how much he has been controlling. There must be some records, if not actual correspondence, somewhere.

"Besides, there are the evidences of Limbrook and his sister. The two together should go a long way toward a conviction, even if they don't get to the end of the road. And Catsgill—by the way, I've just heard from the hospital that he's coming round. They think he's almost out of danger now. What he can tell us, added to what we've found out in Adam Street, ought to put salt on the tail of about the shyest bird that we've ever stalked.

"I was talking this over with Tolbooth just before you came in, and he's of the same opinion. He thinks the way Mildew used Catsgill to interview Miss Wingrove was his worst mistake, though it may have seemed shrewd at the time—would have been, I suppose, if Catsgill hadn't made up his mind to give him away. It proves that Mildew's contact with Limbrook wasn't the innocent, casual matter which he represented to us. And in fact, when you think it out, it's hard to say how it can be got over by the trickiest counsel who ever took a rogue's brief for the sake of a thumping fee.

"I should say that Mildew's been shaking in his shoes from the moment he heard that Catsgill hadn't been thoroughly smashed up. It's more likely than not that he's bolted. He may have decided to do that when he heard that Bolton had failed to kidnap the Limbrook pair. There comes a time when the slimmest scoundrel sees that his luck's out, and his nerve cracks. The fact that he's often been away from his home before doesn't prove that he hasn't bolted this time.

"And, if he has, he may take some catching. He's got money, and the right kind of friends to make it awkward for us. And a bolt-hole all ready for such a crisis, more likely than not.... But we've got to get him. I'm trusting you, Cauldron, for that. It'll be all we've done come to nothing, or very near, if we don't have Mildew in the dock now."

Inspector Cauldron observed that the excitement of the siege and capture of the Adam Street menagerie had had its momentary effect upon the nerves of his superior officer. He had not heard him speak so much, nor so rapidly, before now. But what he said was no less sound in its conclusions for that.

"I should say he's on the run, more likely than not," he agreed. "And if he wasn't before, he will be when he reads tonight's news.

It'll be a pointer, if we find he's cleared the cash out of his bank. But that's one of the things we can't find out before morning. If he's not been startled till tonight, we may catch him there trying to draw funds."

"So you may. But it's more likely that he's got accounts ready for such a jam, where he'll have money he can get at that's deposited in other names."

"That's a bright prospect for me! It seems I'm going to need all the luck that's going before I see him stand up in the right place."

"We always need that, and it's wonderful how often it comes our way."

Inspector Cauldron saw that the superintendent was in an invincibly cheerful mood. He turned the subject by asking for further details of the Adam Street siege than he had yet heard, and while he was gaining this information, Superintendent Backwash's optimism appeared to be supported by the event, when the telephone rang sharply to announce that P.C. Hitchins had an urgent report to make from a police-box in the northwest district.

The constable had seen a man whom he was almost certain was Cornelius Mildew in a taxi, and had felt it to be of importance, in view of the instructions which had been issued, to justify him in leaving his beat and following him in another.

Mr. Mildew, if it were he, had alighted in Blake Terrace, N.W. 15, paid off the vehicle, and gone in at No. 9. What was he to do now?

"Hitchins," Superintendent Backwash replied, "if you're right, it's the best day's work that you've ever done. You're only two minutes from the door now? Then keep the house under observation until Inspector Cauldron arrives.... Cauldron, it looks as though we're on velvet again. Mildew hasn't gone to friends. It sounds more like an assignation address. Of course it's luck. It's luck for Hitchins. But it's the kind that only comes to those who have their eyes open and their wits about them.... You'd better take two or three good men with you. You don't know what you'll find worth picking up."

CHAPTER XX.

THE CAUTION OF INSPECTOR CAULDRON

INSPECTOR CAULDRON made a motion to go, and then turned back from the door. A doubt had entered his mind: "You don't think," he asked, "that Hitchins might have made a mistake?"

"No. He seemed sure." The words were confidently said, but were followed by a shade of uncertainty on the superintendent's face. What did he know of Hitchins? Practically nothing at all. But he knew how many false identifications, from police and public alike, would follow general enquiries for wanted men. Certainly he did not wish to add to the number of unwarranted raids for which explanations might be asked on a later day. He woke to a sudden realization that in the confidence it had given that he was at last in process of rounding up the gang which had so long eluded him, he was failing to exercise the astute caution which had brought him the dignity of a private room and the salary which he now drew. Yet he was of no mind to lose the biggest of the fishes that might be already flopping within the net.

"If it's him," he said, "we can't have any risk that he'll get off."

"If it should be he," Inspector Cauldron replied, with no clearer meaning, though somewhat greater precision of speech, as might be expected of one who had joined the force by the college route, "he won't be likely to bolt from there. It's the place he's chosen for a safe hole more likely than not."

"Perhaps not. Unless he sees he's followed. With Hitchins hanging around, and he as cunning as a cartload of monkeys—"

"There's nothing suspicious in a uniformed man passing along the road. It might be his own beat."

"But he might have spotted that he was followed. He'd be wide awake to the risk of that."

"If he did, he'll have got away before now. That is, if there's any bolthole at the back of the place, and if there isn't...."

"If you're proposing not to interview him, after he's been identified as Mildew by one of our own men, you'll have to give a better reason than you have yet."

Inspector Cauldron saw that, if there were to be any delay, the responsibility of the suggestion was to be placed on him. It had given him time for the clarification of his own inarticulated doubt. It had become a reasoned conviction.

"What I'm thinking," he said, "is that if the man isn't Mildew—and we've got to recognize that possibility—we shall lose nothing by the delay. I don't propose to call other enquiries off.

"But if he is, we've got three possibilities to consider. If he guessed, he'll have got away already, if there's any way by which he could do that unobserved. But, if he hasn't, he'll lie low there till we round him up, or he'll use the place for getting in contact with other members of the gang; and, if we watch the place without being suspected, we may find out who those others are, besides getting more evidence against him than we have yet. And you know we can do with a lot more of that.

"He may have gone there because he thought things were getting too warm, or it may be just a routine visit. But even if it's no more than that, he may change his plan when he reads what's been happening this afternoon. In either case, he's likely to get in touch with some of his subordinates. Probably he's got a telephone there, and it might be interesting to listen in."

Superintendent Backwash looked doubtful. "There may be evidence in that house which would ensure him a fifteen-year sentence, or even a hanging if we could connect him with some of the murders which he must have ordered. He may use the time for destroying whatever incriminating material there is. Have you thought of that?"

"If there were a lot of smoke coming out of the chimney I should advocate as quick a visit as we could make."

"Well, I told you to get Mildew at any cost. I'll leave how you do it to you."

Inspector Cauldron felt this to be as much as he could expect to hear. He went quickly out to direct such dispositions as would make it very difficult indeed for Cornelius Mildew, if it were indeed he, to escape unfollowed; or for any communications to pass in or out of No. 9, Blake Terrace without the knowledge of the police.

CHAPTER XXI.

CORNELIUS MILDEW THINKS TWICE

IT is given to few men (if any) to be sure how they will react to circumstances different from the experiences through which they have already passed. Cornelius Mildew knew himself to have coolness and courage of the kind which will meet emergencies and dominate lesser men. He had been confident in himself and in his sufficiency for any occasions that might arise. But that confidence had been based upon the assumption that his precautions had been too absolute for the shadow of prosecution to cross his path.

Coolly he had planned, and ruthlessly he had issued the orders which, by the base—he would have said basic—impulses of greed and fear had controlled the gang of which he had been the head for some most profitable years.

He was a man, as so many are, who had different standards of conduct for his personal contacts and those unseen events which he would direct or allow.

He would not have drowned a kitten with his own hands, unless the occasion had been of a fantastic urgency, yet he had given the word on five occasions, before the blundering effort to dispose of Reginald Catsgill, which had sent better men than himself and one woman to sudden and violent deaths. There is nothing exceptional here in kind, though there may be in degree. There are many eaters of mutton who would be reluctant to kill a sheep. In all he did he would have said that he acted from necessity, which proverbially allows no choice. Where his safety or prosperity was concerned he had no moral scruples at all.

He had a mathematical mind and a retentive memory, which enabled him to control large transactions accurately without the danger of written records. He would smile inwardly at times at the thought of the utter absence of incriminating documents relating to the criminal activities which gave him so large a share of his present wealth. He relied upon this method of conducting his illicit transactions, not merely as providing negative absence of proof, but as a positive argument which would be of almost invincible strength. To accuse him of controlling transactions of such magnitude in the absence of any documentary records would be to outrage probability to a degree that any competent counsel could demonstrate as absurd.

That was as far as his mind, even in the night hours, would approach the possibility that he might ever be brought to face a criminal charge: a fantasy so remote that he could contemplate its absurd collapse with the aloofness with which a man considers his neighbour's case.

With the leisured, far-sighted care with which all his precautions had been taken, he had built up for himself a character opposite to that on which he relied. He was known among his associates, and particularly at the bridge-table, as a man both generous and careless in his financial methods. His game was competent, without brilliance, so that his partners had little cause for complaint, but, if he should keep the score, he would be quite likely to make errors against himself, which his opponents would correct. There was a bet once that he would settle his liability twice over on a losing afternoon, if he were asked to do so at an interval of not less than an hour, and this bet was won. He had looked bewildered and hesitant for a moment, and then, with a word of apology for his forgetfulness, pulled out his pocket-book, and handed over the seven pounds he had lost before being told that the amount was already paid. If his correspondence should, at any moment, be seized, and his banking accounts probed, there would be nothing to explain beyond the source of much of the money which he possessed; and here, again, his reputation for affluent carelessness should be his sufficient shield. His stock exchange transactions were many. His habit of destroying the record of these, even though of an innocent kind, might easily lead to prolonged investigation of items which would prove to be of that nature, especially as he made a point of being paid, even large sums, by open cheques, which he would cash. Even proof that he had possessed bank-notes of dubious origin should not be an acute danger. He made large bets. His wallet was often stuffed with notes of high values, the source of which he would have professed inability to recall. If it were not beyond reason to assert that such a one as he were in control of an international drug-trafficking gang, why should not another member of his exclusive club be under equal suspicion? Why should not the tainted notes have been passed over in the card room or at the billiard table to a man who was notoriously careless in such matters? And, finally, no man is bound to incriminate himself. If an assertion of integrity, and a profession of forgetfulness might not be enough, absolute silence should prove an impregnable shield.

Perhaps, he had thought, if such questions should arise, as he had felt sure that they never would, subsequent questions of income tax liability would be his greater trouble. But even that might not be much. Gambling losses and gains are beyond the range of British taxation, except upon the earnings of professional bookmakers. And investigation would show not only that he had paid without protest all assessments that had been made upon him, but these had included some items for which he was not liable. It had all been done consistently with the character which he had deliberately assumed and maintained. And yet, suddenly, there had fallen upon him the shadow of urgent fear.

Now he sat in a small back-parlour of No. 9, Blake Terrace, asking himself, as he had done a dozen times before, where and how his elaborate precautions had failed and how serious the occasion might prove to be. He had not fled as yet. It was an extremity he had hardly brought himself to contemplate. He did not yet know of the events that had enlivened Adam Street during the afternoon. But he knew that Catsgill was still alive, and that the attempt to kidnap Limbrook and his sister had been frustrated by the action of that young woman, whose wits had not been adequately recognised by his agents on that and at least one earlier occasion. They had blundered badly. But that should have involved him in no danger. He had always foreseen and discounted such possibilities. It was the incalculable chance of the Limbrook episode, the malice of unpredictable circumstance, which had threatened his cultured peace. That was the conclusion to which he had always come and which gave him some confidence. He told himself that he had not blundered. He had no occasion to blame himself. He had only to rely on nerves which had not failed him yet, and he should be equal to the event.... Catsgill's intended treachery would not have disturbed his mind had it stood alone. And, even now, the precautions he had taken before ordering that abortive "accident" might be all that the occasion required. Certainly he would not condemn himself by the folly of flight unless there should be more menace than he now saw.... At the worst, he could get, provide, and forfeit bail.... But this was absurd! The police might have had their suspicions directed toward himself, and there was enough annoyance in that. But the degree of proof which a prosecution requires is a far different matter.

For the moment there was nothing more to be done. He had ordered that Limbrook and his sister should be destroyed, by whatever means, as soon as they should be traced. That might be accomplished at any moment. It might be done now. He would hear of it, after that, in a safe and convenient way. But not necessarily at once. Continual contacts with even the highest of his subordinates were no part of his wary methods. Having given the order, he assumed that it would be executed. Only blunders and failures—and those only of the most serious—would be brought to him. Men such as Bolton would not even know the name of him from whom their orders derived. They could not betray that which they did not know.

As to Catsgill, he had said that nothing should be done for a time, let the man say what he would. A second attempt upon his life would be too dangerous. It would destroy the construction of accident. If it were worthwhile to murder Catsgill to shut his mouth, it amounted to an admission that the lawyer's allegations were dangerous, and therefore founded on truth, and who knew what he might already have dictated—signed—sworn—from his hospital bed? His turn would come later, either at a quieter or a more urgent day.

But there were matters which Boyle had in hand. Orders would be issued by him to those who would not continue to fail.... It would be amusing to think of Limbrook in the efficient disposal of Maurice Beal. As to Miss Wingrove, his mind turned delicately aside from contemplating the end of a young woman he had rather liked. But his decision did not therefore falter. If a favourite horse should have glanders, who would hesitate to have it shot and its body burned? That which is necessary must be done.

He sat back from a simple meal, but one which it had been no privation to face. There was no doubt that Martha cooked a good chop.

CHAPTER XXII.

Inspector Cauldron Risks Being Thrown Out

AROUND Blake Terrace Inspector Cauldron cast a wide net, but its meshes were small. He had interviewed Constable Hitchins, and satisfied himself that the identification, if less than certain, was more than a random guess. This being so, he had good hope that he had Mildew within his grasp, and, if so, he did not intend that he should escape.

But he argued that if he were intending flight he would probably remain for a time within walls where, if he had not been seen to enter, he could never be suspected to be; but that otherwise he would leave a house which could have few comforts or attractions for him within a few hours; and he gave instructions that, should he do so, he should be followed, but not arrested until his identification had been confirmed, and he had either led his trailers to another secret resort or returned to his accustomed environment. In either case, he need not know that his visit to Blake Terrace had been observed, and more of his associates, if not of himself, might be learned by continual watching of that innocent-looking suburban residence.

Innocent-seeming it certainly was, and investigation of its reputed tenant did nothing to reduce this inoffensive aspect. There was time enough for this, for the night passed, and the morning came, and none but the inevitable tradespeople approached a door from which no one emerged. The books of the rating authorities showed that the house had been occupied for many years by Mrs. Martha Braddock, the widow of a naval officer, in whose name the house had stood until his death fourteen years before. He had been of good family and unblemished record, and his widow's reputation was good in the negative sense that she did nothing which drew the attention of the police.

112

Desiring to know more than that, and obtaining the chance information that she attended the parish church, Inspector Cauldron interviewed the vicar, with a discreet economy of explanation which left a vague impression on the clerical gentleman's mind that the police wished to identify the lady with a missing heir, but were anxious that their enquiries should not be known to her, lest disappointment should follow.

An expansive man of a bald-headed urbanity, by no means deficient in common sense or worldly experience, he described the lady as being of good character and discretion. Kindly, practical, sharp-tongued at times, but generous to deserving need. If he made appeal to her he could rely on her cheque-book being brought out. But the subscription would not be large. Her means, he supposed, were not very great. On the other hand, large anonymous donations had been received from time to time for the Church Restoration Fund and other religious or philanthropic objects which—but for that reputation of limited income—he would have suspected to come from her.

She lived quietly, keeping one maid. She occasionally had small social gatherings connected with church activities at her house, which were popular, for she entertained well. He particularly approved her scones.

Inspector Cauldron, digesting this information as he left the vicarage, wondered whether he were wasting his time. It seemed likely enough. But, at the worst, it was no more than that. The search for Cornelius Mildew in other directions was not being relaxed. And in one particular he was encouraged by the negative evidence of these most innocent facts. Constable Hitchins might be wrong in his identification, but that the man he had followed had entered Mrs. Braddock's house was a fact to which he would swear emphatically. And what male visitor should such a lady have, who calls in the afternoon and has not emerged again when next morning comes?

There was mystery here which sustained hope. But, beyond that, Inspector Cauldron did not deny to himself that the lady's record—too long established to be an assumed character to cover illicit deeds since she had become acquainted with Mildew—made it improbable that her house was used by him for any criminal contacts. There was only the hint of large anonymous charities to confuse the picture. Mildew gave to charities with a free hand. It would be according to his technique. But to do it with so careful an anonymity that even the vicar had been left in doubt? No, he could see no purpose in that.

He interviewed the vicar at 10:00 A.M. Within an hour of that time he was back at Scotland Yard, to enquire whether there had been any emergence from the watched house. He learned that there was still nothing to report. No one had entered or left. The telephone operator who, with very dubious legality, was tapping the lady's wire, reported that she had ordered a leg of lamb from her usual butcher. Did that suggest that there were more than herself and her maid to sit down to meat? Scarcely. She had emphasized that it must be a small leg.

Superintendent Backwash, still basking in the glory of the Adam Street raid, listened to the inspector's account of his vicarage call, and said no more than: "Well, that's that. What are you going to do now?"

Inspector Cauldron understood that the batting was left to him, and that, if he should fail in this, the first important case which had been allotted to him, it might be a long time before such an opportunity would be his again. But he did not intend to fail. He had more ideas than time to translate them to action. He said: "Mildew must use someone, and some address, for clearing cheques, and dealing with all the cash that goes through his hands. Why shouldn't he do it there? I thought of calling on the local inspector of taxes and perhaps getting a sight of Mrs. Braddock's returns. You don't know what pointer they might give."

"I should say that's a poor chance. But it won't make any difference because you won't see anything. You'll get shown the door."

"I don't see why he shouldn't be willing to help."

"Well, he won't. I don't say it's never been done, but it can't be managed from our end. The Home Secretary'd have to get to work first."

"Well, there's no harm in trying."

"Not if you don't mind being kicked out. When do you propose to ring the Blake Terrace bell? You couldn't get anything worse than a kick there."

"I'm in no hurry to do that, because, unless we get a search warrant, I don't see what we should gain. Say Mrs. Braddock comes to the door. Or the maid. If they're screwy they'll know what to do. I should walk down the steps no wiser, but have just upped them off to be on the alert. And if everything's all right—well, we draw a blank either way. It's a cat-and-mouse business, and we want the mouse to feel safe enough to come out for a walk."

"We couldn't easily get a search warrant. I've been discussing that with the Commissioner. We've too little to go on; and what you've found out about the lady's good character puts that further back."

"That's how I figured it."

"But when you've been thrown out by the I.O.T. you'd better come back here. Say at two-thirty. I might have a surprise for you then…. No, I can't say anything more now. One thing at a time's a good rule."

Knowing when there would be no profit in further words, Inspector Cauldron went.

He called upon the inspector of taxes, a Mr. Peter Belfrey, a tall, thin, fair-haired man with a drawling politeness of manner with which he encountered equally the varied multitudinous victims of every social grade of the district which it was his duty to farm. His slowness of speech gave time for the operation of wits which moved at a better pace: his indifferent unemotional aloofness of manner was a barrier against which anger, rudeness, protest, or pleading of any tone were equally impotent.

But Inspector Cauldron had a cause for hope which he had not mentioned under the provocation of Superintendent Backwash's derisive forecasts. "If," he said to himself, "it's the Pete Belfrey I knew at school, and Belfrey isn't a common name—" And when he was shown into the tax inspector's private room he saw that the same Pete Belfrey it was. He would have known him at once, even without the tie which the inspector of taxes continued to wear, but the inspector of the C.I.D. had discarded lest it should make him unpopular among colleagues whose education had been at less widely reputed schools.

Mr. Belfrey looked at the name on the card, glanced in his aloof speculative manner at the face of his visitor, and then said with some human warmth, though a shade of doubt in his voice: "C. T. Cauldron? Not Cecil? Not Cecil by any chance?"

As he spoke the eyes of the two men met, and the doubt was gone. "I ought," he said, "to have been sure at the first glance. But who'd have thought of meeting you in the C.I.D.?"

"We didn't all get the same opportunities among which to choose."

If Mr. Belfrey observed any implication in this riposte he showed no sign, and his reply, when it came, was neatly adequate to the occasion: "Oh, I wasn't meaning you'd got any reason to envy me. The boot's on the other leg. You'll be known all over the world when I'm a retired nonentity with nothing but a few enemies in my last district to remember that such a man ever lived. But, apart from that, and your job being more exciting, I shouldn't say there's much difference in the kind of work we've chosen."

"I hoped you'd look at it like that. I've got a puzzling problem to solve, and it's one where you might give me a bit of help, which I felt sure you'd be glad to do."

"So I should; though I wouldn't say I'm likely to be much use. What's the trouble?"

Inspector Cauldron became eloquent. He told at length the tale of the Yard's vain attempts to break up the Mildew Gang or reach those who were at the head of its operations. He did not omit the curious incident of the arrest of Eustace Limbrook, nor the events arising therefrom—which had raised hopes of ending its activities—hopes which were near to realization or frustration now.

It was a tale to which any man may listen without going to sleep, and Mr. Belfrey was accustomed to patient hearing of duller matters. He said at its conclusion: "It just shows which of us has got into the better job. You've been put on to a game like this, while I was listening for the best part of an hour before you came to a man who wanted me to believe that his firm spent nearly two thousand pounds in travelling expenses, while they've only got two men on the road.... But what is it you want me to do for you?"

"I thought you might give me a hint as to whether there are any large funds—more than her own estate, which is probably a quite moderate amount—in her name. I don't suppose that that could happen without it coming under the notice of your department from one angle or other."

"I'm sorry; but I couldn't possibly do anything of the kind."

"Or if you could merely tell me that there's nothing suspicious in her accounts. That might do her a good turn rather than not, as it might save enquiries in other directions."

Mr. Belfrey permitted himself a slight smile. "And if I undertook to do that, and then said I.... In fact, you've got into the right groove. You ought to go a lot further than I ever shall."

"Of course, it would be absolutely confidential. You know me well enough to—"

"Quite. Though you mightn't find it an easy promise to keep. But there's nothing doing. Nothing," he repeated with the smiling drawl which disguised the final quality of the words, "nothing doing at all."

"I wonder whether you've thought of the fearful harm these drug traffickers do. We say at the Yard that if its ten years for them, a common murderer ought to get off with a month's hard."

"No, I can't say I have. I'll think about it, if you like; and if I can give you a leg up after office hours you can count on me. But it's no use asking me to betray the confidence the taxpayer gives the state, which I'm under oath that I won't do."

Inspector Cauldron considered this. There was nothing in his memories of Pete Belfrey to give him hope that further argument would avail. He got up, said a few words on personal topics, and retired defeated.

CHAPTER XXIII.

BILLIE TAKES A TOUGH JOB

INSPECTOR CAULDRON kept his two-thirty appointment at Superintendent Backwash's office in a chastened mood. He was less interested in the revelation which the superintendent had promised than in his own failure, which had been so confidently foretold and which he must now report. Probably what Superintendent Backwash really thought was that he had been wasting his time, as a more experienced officer would have been unlikely to do!

But he did not have to bring up the subject; it was brought up to him. "So you've been thrown out?" the superintendent began as he entered the room, in a voice in which derision and good humour were about equally blended.

Inspector Cauldron endeavoured to answer in the same voice: "No. Not thrown. Shown would be the more accurate word."

"Make your own choice! There's another detective anxious to take on this Mildew job, and the Commissioner's left it to me to decide."

"You don't mean you're going to let someone else take it over now!" Bitterness, resentment, and a surprise which was almost incredulity contended in the exclamation. But the superintendent was his superior officer, and, if that decision had been made, from whatever cause, it must be accepted with as little evidence of feeling as he could contrive.

Superintendent Backwash heard him without changing the expression of good humour that was almost a grin. It approached indecency. Inspector Cauldron realized that there might have been some development during the morning which had demonstrated him to be incompetent and would justify so important an investigation being transferred to a senior officer. Yet what possible source of amusement could there be in that?

But the words which followed turned his thoughts to a different issue and to protest of another kind.

"We've had Miss Wingrove here since you went out. She says she's done well enough to merit a regular job. The question is, shall we let her in on the Mildew case?"

"I hope you told her it's no woman's work. She's been in danger enough."

"Which she's come through with a good nerve. We took a statement from Mr. Catsgill this morning. We've had her interview with him from his angle, and he gives her high praise. Very high indeed. I thought there might have been colleagues you'd be less willing to have."

This was an aspect of the matter which had already risen above the horizon of Inspector Cauldron's thoughts, with an enlivening effect which he felt bound to disregard.

"I wasn't looking at it like that," he said. "I think it's too much danger for her."

"That depends on what we let her do, doesn't it? And what protection she has from us? She's been in danger enough doing things on her own, particularly in the Adam Street business yesterday. The fact is, as you know, we did let her work for us before that; and if she asks to go on, and be put in a regular position, it's not easy to refuse."

"I think you ought to, all the same. What does Mr. Limbrook say about it?"

"I don't know that she's asked him, or why she should. But, in fact, she says he's rather more badly burned than we understood yesterday. It's likely to be a week or more before he's walking again."

"I'm sorry to hear that. But as to her being involved—"

"Well, nothing's settled yet. She's waiting to hear our decision now. You know her best, and you seem to have a very strong conviction of her incapacity—"

"I didn't say that. What I meant—"

"You didn't exactly say it, but you expressed yourself so strongly that it was evident that you've no confidence that she could take care of herself. I think it might be the best way to have her in."

He touched his bell, and next moment Billie was shown into the room.

She shook hands with Inspector Cauldron (whom she had not seen since he drove her to Croydon aerodrome under the impression that she was about to fly to Scotland to be her half-brother's bride), greeting him with friendly eyes. But they changed to another mood when Superintendent Backwash said: "I'm afraid we can't see our way to putting you on to the Mildew case now, Miss Wingrove. There may not be very much to do which would come within your range. I can't be sure about that yet—and the case has been given to Inspector Cauldron, who doesn't think you are suitable to be any further assistance to him."

The words were not such as Inspector Cauldron would have chosen, and yet they were hard to deny unless he would withdraw the protest he had made, which he was unwilling to do.

Billie looked at him with surprised and resentful eyes. "I don't see why," she exclaimed, "he should say that! You said yourself this morning that I had been of real use, and you'd done some things which would have been impossible if I hadn't helped."

"So I did. I said we were grateful, particularly for what happened yesterday; and that we should be glad to show it in some more tangible form than we have yet done.

"But there's only one thing that I care to ask. Can't you understand that if anyone starts in at anything they may like seeing it through?"

"Yes. I can understand that. But I thought you asked for something more than being in on the Mildew affair. I thought you wanted a regular position on the staff of the C.I.D."

"So I do. I'm sure I should like the work. But it's the Mildew business about which I'm particularly keen. I feel I'm doing something worthwhile if I'm helping to break up such a gang as that."

Inspector Cauldron broke into the conversation with: "Do you mean only yourself, or is Mr. Limbrook wanting to be in this too?"

"Only myself. Mr. Limbrook has his profession. And he's laid up now, as you know. I haven't mentioned it to him."

"I was only wondering what he'll say when you do."

"I don't suppose it'll be anything very dreadful." Billie's lips curved to a smile as she said this. After all, she wasn't accountable to Eustace! But she wasn't going to speak slightingly of him to Inspector Cauldron, especially while he was in this very unpleasant mood. Her eyes moved enquiringly from one to the other. It seemed that the decision lay with them, and while she was confident that she could manage either of them alone, the dual problem might be more complicated.

"Of course," she said, "if you'd rather I work separately, and just call you in at the last moment, as Eustace did yesterday—"

"You know, Miss Wingrove," Inspector Cauldron replied, "I don't wish anything of the sort. I think you ought to be content with what you've done already. We're dealing with a wealthy and most dangerous gang, most of whom we don't even know with certainty, but we know they're high up, and that they'll stick at nothing—murder included—if they think we're getting too close to them. It's touch and go, even now, as to whether we get them at all."

"Inspector Cauldron," the superintendent interposed blandly, "has had a disappointing morning. It makes him look on the black side of everything. After a night's sleep—"

"I'm sorry for that," Billie said, with a quick change of mood. "I hope it wasn't anything serious."

Explanation followed. Inspector Cauldron, who disliked quarrelling with her almost as much as the idea of her risking her safety in further skirmishes with an unscrupulous foe, was glad to turn the conversation to a detailed account of his interview with Mr. Belfrey, and a frank admission of his failure to overcome the official rectitude of his schooldays' friend. While he spoke the superintendent had an idea. He had some confidence in Miss Wingrove's capacity, and he neither wished to reject the assistance she had offered, nor to force it upon Inspector Cauldron against his will. He asked: "Do you think he'd have given the information if Miss Wingrove had approached him in a different way?"

"No," Inspector Cauldron answered confidently, "I'm sure he wouldn't. Belfrey isn't that sort."

He had a memory of Peter in earlier years. He rarely even looked at a girl! And he was about as unlikely to be tricked or wheedled into disclosing official secrets as any man he had ever known.

"Well, then," the superintendent asked, "shall we say, if Miss Wingrove can manage that, she shall have the job?"

"Yes, I don't mind that, if Miss Wingrove's really willing to take it on."

Billie, reacting to the scepticism in his voice, replied with a confidence which she did not feel, and which would diminish further in the next hour. She said, with a clarity of meaning which must be its grammar's excuse: "I should say it would be about the easiest thing that I ever did."

CHAPTER XXIV.

Heroine Becomes Thief

BILLIE said: "I'd better go now, and get the job done. What exactly is it you want?"

"I wanted," Inspector Cauldron replied, "to get all the information I could about Mrs. Braddock's investments, and, if possible, where she banks, and what income she has."

"I hope," the superintendent interposed with belated caution, "that you won't do anything of an irregular kind. We couldn't countenance that."

"You mean something like starting a fire and stealing the file in the confusion that would be sure to follow? Well, that's an idea. And since yesterday I feel I know all about fires! But you needn't worry. I'm not acting for you. Not till I've finished this."

"So long as it's understood that, if you get into any jam, you mustn't expect us to get you out."

"I shan't say a word. Not even when you run me in after you find Mr. Belfrey with a pitchfork stuck in his back."

"Very well, then I'll wish you luck."

"And I can't have too much of that."

With these words, Billie went out, having a slip of paper on which Inspector Cauldron had written Mr. Belfrey's address in her hand, and a sinking heart which she did not wish these annoying policemen to guess.

"I've no idea," she thought, "how I shall get over this Mr. Belfrey. I expect tax collectors are perfectly beastly men. But if I put it off, I shall feel more jittery than I do now."

She looked at her watch. It was 3:23. She had a well-founded idea that the offices of inspectors of taxes are closed to the public at an early hour. She looked round for an appropriate bus.

Twenty minutes later she stood at a mahogany counter divided by glazed partitions, so that protestants against the rapacity of the State could be interviewed with a veneer of privacy, the reality of which must depend upon the restraints of their own voices and their neighbours' eyes. She was reminded of the reception arrangements in the "Loan Department" of the shop of Messrs. Nathan and Aaronsberg in New Oxford Street, where she had parted with her mother's engagement ring—the only valuable piece of jewellery which she possessed—in exchange for the temporary use of seven pounds, on the two occasions when her irregular income had failed to provide the minimum which credit cannot obtain, and for which abstinence is no remedy.

A young clerk, neatly nondescript, advanced. "Can I see Mr. Belfrey?" she enquired before he could ask the business on which she came.

The embryo tax inspector was diplomatic: "I'm afraid Mr. Belfrey is engaged. Can I do anything for you?"

Billie observed the disadvantage of having no official status. She felt sure that Inspector Cauldron's card had been potent to secure an interview without this preliminary obstruction. She remembered the exclamation of the Turkish general at the siege of Malta when his troops recoiled from St. Elmo's guns: "If we cannot slay the calf, how shall we deal with the cow?"

She favoured the waiting calf with her brightest smile as she answered: "I'm afraid not. It's a matter on which I must see Mr. Belfrey himself."

"What name shall I give him?"

Billie produced her card. It was a business one, announcing her as a research worker.

The calf looked at it with an expressionless face and an inward doubt. He was not very clear about the lady's profession, but he was more interested in her address. It was not in Mr. Belfrey's district. In fact, it was miles out! Nor did he recall the name of Wilhelmina Wingrove among the many files which he kept so neatly arranged. The lady might be no more than a canvasser for some charitable or cultural cause. He said: "I'm afraid Mr. Belfrey will want to know on what business you wish to see him."

"It isn't business. Not taxes. Not exactly, I mean. It's a personal matter."

This hesitant denial (for her mind was obstructed by an inopportune question—was it taxes or wasn't it? Yes or no?) put the clerk in a fresh doubt. Probably a personal plea for leniency for herself or others for time to pay, when the local collector was putting pressure upon a defaulter, as it was his duty to do! But, on the other hand, the lady might be a personal friend of his principal, to whom courtesy could be wisely paid. Card in hand, he turned with no further words, and disappeared within the door of Mr. Belfrey's private office.

Coming out, he went back to his own desk, giving no sign of the result of his mission; but next moment Mr. Belfrey's door opened and he appeared, showing a visitor out, to whom he was speaking with the guarded cordiality that one professional man gives to another. Anyone more experienced than Billie would have recognized that it was not a victim in person, but his accountant or lawyer, who was being dismissed in that manner.

But Billie was indifferent to anything but the difficult and lawless mission on which she had come. Her eyes were upon Mr. Belfrey, appraising her unconscious opponent. She was no victim of his assessments, but one who intended that victimization should be in the opposite direction.

After all, he might not be very formidable! She could tell better when she had looked into his eyes.... Now he was looking at her. She saw that her card was in his hand. But he did not invite her into his office, as she had expected him to do. He came forward to where she stood, on her own side of the partitioned counter. His voice was polite, but with the official distance that men in his position must practise to keep, as he asked: "You wish to see me?"

"Yes, if you could spare a few minutes."

He saw that she did not propose to state her business as they stood there. With only momentary hesitation, he said: "Come this way," and showed her, stepping aside with the same formal politeness, into his private room.

"I wanted," she said at once as she sat down before nervousness could assert itself to delay her words, "to see you about the Mildew matter—about what Inspector Cauldron called to see you about this morning."

It was not well expressed, but it was no less dear for that. Mr. Belfrey looked at the card again. He looked at Billie in a more personal way than he had yet done. He asked: "Do you mean that you are from Scotland Yard?"

The question allowed of diverse replies. She said: "I've just come from there, if you mean that.... The fact is," she added, with a sudden impulse of candour, "they won't let me go on helping them unless I can get you to tell them what they want to know."

Mr. Belfrey looked puzzled at this, but with nothing in his expression to indicate that he would be likely to yield. Then his face cleared to a sudden realization of who his visitor must be. Yes, that was the name! Adding what he had read in the Press concerning the Adam Street fire to the more extended narrative with which Inspector Cauldron had endeavoured to win his interest, he looked at her with a friendliness, even an admiration, which roused a hope that she might not be destined to fail.

Mr. Belfrey's thought was that he had not expected the heroine of Cauldron's tale to be of such attractive appearance. He understood now why Cauldron had become almost lyrical at times in his narrative of the assistance which Miss Wingrove had rendered to the police. But Cauldron always had been a bit on the sentimental side. Mr. Belfrey's own observation was that the world's amazons are not distinguished by physical charm. He remembered suffragists—"suffragettes" it had been usual to call them, a word probably coined by some illiterate journalist for the maddening of those who respect language, but how congenial it must have become to the BBC!—taking tea at his mother's house. No one would have fallen for *them*. But Miss Wingrove was pleading now with words to which he gave less heed than to the eloquence of her eyes.

"I feel sure," he replied, "that you will understand, Miss Wingrove, that I would help you if I could. But, as I told Inspector Cauldron, it is not a matter concerning which I have any discretionary power. I don't think the police are treating you quite fairly in sending you on such an errand."

Billie agreed to that. "I don't think it was fair at all. But you know what the police are! I mightn't have come, only that, from the way Inspector Cauldron spoke of you, I felt sure you'd think of some way of helping me out."

"I'm afraid you felt a confidence which I can do nothing to justify. I'm sorry, but—" As he spoke, he touched his bell. "Smithers," he said to the clerk who answered: "Fetch Mrs. Martha Braddock's file. She's at 9, Blake Terrace."

Next minute the file was upon his desk. Silently he studied its contents for some moments, while Billie waited, uncertain what it could mean, and unable to persuade herself that she had so easily won.

It was an incredulity which lessened her disappointment when he closed it with the words: "I'm sorry, but however much I may sympathize personally with what you are trying to do, in my official capacity I have no right to give you any information at all."

Billie felt that the words were no worse than she had expected to hear. And yet, if he had no other purpose, why had he sent for the file? Was it not because, had its contents been of a nature to clear Mrs. Braddock from suspicion of any connection with the finances of the gang, he might, in some carefully chosen, literally defensible words, have given her that hint, so that she would have been content to abandon a barren quest, and even to satisfy the police that her mission had not failed?

A conviction that this was the case redoubled an obstinacy which had already resolved that it would be no easy task to persuade her to leave the room till she had gained her illegal end. For was not the inference clear that there was some damning evidence in that file, which had rendered it impossible for Mr. Belfrey to speak the absolving word?

It was a presumption which his next sentence converted to certainty, for when she said, with a smiling pertinacity which was determined neither to lose temper nor admit defeat, "You know I can't possibly go back and tell Superintendent Backwash no more than that! It means such a lot to me!" he replied, with a measured gravity of language which told her that she was listening to more than a general statement of official procedure: "You are at liberty to tell the police this. Though we may be restricted in what we say, it is no less our duty to listen to what we hear, from whatever source. You may be sure that the suggestion of Inspector Cauldron and yourself will be impartially examined, and any other than a negative result will be laid before the proper authorities at a proper time and in a proper way."

"And what good would that be then! Even if the proper authorities—whoever they are—wouldn't take the same line, and find out that it would take an Act of Parliament to open their mouths? If it doesn't make you all accessories to crime, it must be a near thing! If you would only think of all the dreadful harm that these people do!"

She had a last desperate thought. "If you'll tell me who the authority is, I'll go and see him at once. There can't be anything gained by delay, and, after what you've said I could tell him, I *know* there's something fishy in the woman's returns."

She thought that, if she could go back with nothing better than the name of a higher official to whom application could be made by the police, it might be argued that she had not utterly failed. But her last words had been taken more seriously than she had foreseen.

"If you should make such a statement, Miss Wingrove, it would be utterly unwarranted by anything I had said, and might—if it were believed, which I should think improbable—be most detrimental to me.

"You must be more foolish than I had supposed if you think I would give you an introduction which could be used for such a purpose.

"But in fact, the procedure would be quite irregular. I am supposed to be equal to dealing with my own callers and making my own reports."

"I'm sorry. I am really. I know I ought not to have said it, and it wouldn't have been a right thing to do. But if you can't give me an introduction, there must be someone you could ring up and ask."

Mr. Belfrey made no immediate answer to this. He turned a pencil over upon his desk. He drew on his pad. Billie, watching in an expectant silence, saw a swallow develop, with outstretched wings. There were others upon the pad. Did their creation assist thought? Were they supposed to be catching flies on the wing, as swallows certainly do? And were the flies the tax payers of the district Mr. Belfrey controlled?

Resisting an impulse to raise this interesting but inopportune question, she waited for the inspector of taxes to have the next word.

"It won't be the least possible good, but, if it's not too late in the afternoon, I don't mind telephoning to report on the allegation—if it can be said to amount to that—which you and the police have made, and I'll let you know what reply I get—that is, if it should not be of a confidential kind. But I shall telephone from the next room, and I must ask you not to make any attempt to overhear what I shall say."

"Yes. I'll promise that."

Mr. Belfrey appeared to take her word without hesitation, but when he had opened the door, and looked out upon the larger office, which his clerks had now left for the day, and added, "You mustn't get impatient if I am some minutes. I shall be speaking with a gentleman with whom I cannot expect to be connected at once," he closed the door carefully as he went out.

Billie considered that heavy door. Certainly no sound of speaking would penetrate its massive panels or beneath its thickly carpeted edge. She had been told no more than to stay there, and that he would be some minutes away.

She looked at the file which still lay on the broad desk, six feet from her hand, in front of his vacant chair. *Had he meant that?* She did not—she would never—know. She remembered the superintendent's warning and her own lightly worded retort. Was she about to do something supremely silly as well as indisputably wrong? She did not know; but she knew that the occasion was too good to miss. She rose, reached over, and drew the file to her own side of the table.

After all, she would only look. She would take nothing away....

It was fully five minutes before Mr. Belfrey returned. He said, in his more formal manner: "I am sorry, Miss Wingrove, but the rules of secrecy which it is our sworn duty to observe cannot be broken on such a pretext as has been proposed. It was my original view, and has now been emphatically confirmed."

He had gone round to his desk as he spoke, and stood there, not resuming his seat. His eyes were upon the file. Had she replaced it exactly? Surely there was no difference he could observe?

She said, with a nervous smile: "I think you draw swallows beautifully, Mr. Belfrey."

He answered in an absent-minded manner, though giving no sign of his thoughts: "Perhaps they look best when they are upside down."

He may have noticed that she had not seemed much concerned at the refusal he had given her. She blamed herself afterwards for the clumsiness of that omission. Would she always make these amateur blunders in the paths of duplicity which she had become so strangely willing to tread?

But he said no more than: "I am sure, Miss Wingrove, that I can rely upon you not to misrepresent anything that has passed between us. You will appreciate my position as well as yours."

Did those grave slow words mean that he guessed? It was certain he could not know. Yet.

Calling upon all her courage she raised her eyes to meet his with their usual frankness. "You can be quite sure about that."

"It is what," he answered, "I should he very foolish to doubt."

It was a parting of friends.

CHAPTER XXV.

BILLIE WILL COLLECT

LEAVING Mr. Belfrey's office, Billie looked round for a taxi. She aimed to be back at New Scotland Yard at the first minute she could, and, if possible, before Superintendent Backwash should have left for the day.

About Inspector Cauldron's presence she was less particular. She felt her victory to be over him, and it was a feeling very pleasant to have; but even in this moment of elation he was no more than half forgiven for the difficulties he had made. He could wait his turn. But the superintendent was the one whose promise she had and who had power to give her the position she coveted. It was for him she asked, and to his room she was promptly shown. But when she entered she found that Inspector Cauldron was also there.

"Mr. Belfrey," she said at once, "is very sorry, but he can't tell us anything. He's an example of official rectitude—or would correctitude be the word?—you couldn't easily beat."

"So you learnt nothing?" It was the superintendent who asked. Her words had been definite, but her looks, in spite of demure control, were not those of one whom failure depressed, and neither of the experienced officers to whom she spoke was entirely deceived.

"I learnt a lot," she said, "about the official mind."

"I expect you did. But not about Mrs. Braddock's investments?"

"Well, I've had an idea. If she had large sums to invest they'd be in public companies' shares or debentures more likely than not?"

"Yes. Or Government stocks. It's not certain, but it's quite probable."

"And you could get to see the lists of their shareholders?"

"Theoretically, yes. But if you're proposing that we should search all the files at Somerset House!" There was a sarcastic note in the superintendent's voice as he said this, of which she must have been aware, but Inspector Cauldron, watching with a growing perception that there was more to come, noticed that her cheerfulness did not lessen. It may have been the same consciousness, and the belief that he now knew the paltriness of the idea on which she had relied, which caused the superintendent to add: "We might have thought of that for ourselves, Miss Wingrove, even though we were twice as dumb as you think we are."

"I don't think you're dumb at all. Not when talking pays. But I see the point. Searching might take rather a long time, if you'd no good ideas as to where to look. But suppose you thought that some companies would be more likely than others?"

As she spoke she opened her bag and drew out a sheet of paper, which she passed across the superintendent's desk. "I thought these might be quite good for a start."

The superintendent saw about a dozen names scribbled on the back of a shopping bill. He considered them for a moment, observing that while some were universally known, two or three would be familiar to few outside professional and investment circles. He looked up to say: "There's no guessing here, Miss Wingrove. Where did you get this?"

"I got it from Debenham and Freebody's. You see, when I came back to London, I left all my luggage behind. I had to buy almost everything."

"You know I didn't mean that."

"I've always understood that making statements gets people into a mess, and sometimes others as well, even though it may help the police."

"That's what you're supposed to be doing now."

Inspector Cauldron spoke for the first time: "I suppose, Miss Wingrove, you didn't take Mr. Belfrey's first refusal as final?"

"No, of course not. But he didn't change it, if you mean that. I got him so far that he phoned someone over him, but he only got told to bang the door a bit louder than he'd been doing before. He wouldn't even let me hear what he said. He went into the next room; for that. He was away quite a while."

A moment's silence followed this guileless statement. The two police officers exchanged looks of dawning comprehension, but, as Billie had said, they knew when to be dumb.

"The question is," she said, after that pregnant pause, "what you're going to do for me?"

"If this list," the superintendent replied; "is as much use as I feel sure it will be, there won't be any doubt about that."

Billie's cheerfulness dimpled into a full smile. See saw (but had she not been sure from when she entered the room?) that the game was won.

"In that case," she said, "the question is: what am I to do next?"

"You don't lose much time, Miss Wingrove. Have you any ideas on that subject yourself?"

"It did occur to me that a call on Mrs. Braddock couldn't do any harm."

"In what capacity, and with what intention, should you do that?"

"It wouldn't much matter what, so long as she doesn't guess why. I might see more inside than your men can from the other side of the gate. And I could find out what sort of a woman she really is."

"Yes," the superintendent agreed, though with some doubt in his voice, "if there's no one there who'll guess that you come from us."

"I don't see why they should. If Mildew's there, he'll be sure to be somewhere out of sight. He won't open the door. I might go canvassing for something, or collecting for a charity she'd be inclined to support."

Superintendent Backwash reflected that the two calls which Billie had made already—those upon the respectable Belfrey and the less reputable Beal—had not been barren of consequence. His mind went further back, and recalled others of more or less equal fruitfulness. He saw doubt in Inspector Cauldron's eyes, and he decided to let her go. He could not honestly tell himself that there was no risk involved. They were dealing with a man who was known to be ruthless and might be desperate now. If she should be recognized, the sequel might be seriously unpleasant, even dangerous, for her. But it was her own choice. And if Inspector Cauldron could not avoid looking black every time that—

"Yes," he said, "I think, as we've decided not to raid the house till we know more, it may be worth trying. But you've done enough for today. And morning will be a better time for the kind of call that you have in mind. You'll need to think it over carefully, and be prepared for anything that you're likely to meet. About eleven will be the best time."

"Yes. I'll do that. But I don't suppose it'll make much difference. Things never turn out like you think they will. If you don't want me any more now, I'll go back. It's just occurred to me that I haven't had any tea."

THE RETURN OF THE MILDEW GANG, BY S. FOWLER WRIGHT

"If you think," the superintendent said, as she closed the door, "that that young woman can't be sent anywhere without being marked 'Fragile, with care,' you'd better tell her to clear out at once. But I reckon she's a bit better than that."

CHAPTER XXVI.

Mr. Mildew Had Made a Friend

MRS. MARTHA BRADDOCK was, as the police had correctly learned, the widow of a naval officer who had died as the result of wounds received in action on the China station. Having no inclination for a second marriage, a moderate but sufficient income, sound health, and a disposition of some continuing energy, she had supplemented the ordering of her quiet home by interesting herself in the activities of her parish church and some local charitable organizations.

Being neither quarrelsome nor assertive, she had made few enemies, even among the lady members of the committees on which she sat. Her life had been of a sober eventless integrity, and the voice of scandal had passed her by. It might be thought that few things could be more improbable than that she should be associated with criminal practices of whatever kind.

It had been shortly before her husband's death, and while on a Mediterranean cruise which had been intended to re-establish his damaged health, that she had first met Cornelius Mildew, and shortly after her bereavement that he had called upon her, after making a telephone appointment with some formality, and solicited her assistance.

He was, he explained, a very wealthy man. He had neither wife nor children. He desired to do good during his lifetime rather than leave everything to be spent after his death in ways which he could not control. He desired also (there he admitted some selfishness in himself, which was easier to regret than to overcome) to avoid acquiring the reputation of being a philanthropist to a degree which would surround him with importunities. If Mrs. Braddock could realize the extent to which those who had the reputation of affluence suffered in this way, even without special cause!

To be brief, what he asked, with more circumstance and circumlocution of phrase, and to which, after some interval of consideration, she agreed, was that he should place a sum of twenty thousand pounds in her hands to be invested in her name, on the understanding that the income it produced should be devoted to such charitable causes as she might decide, normally in consultation with him, though this was not an explicit condition. The principal also was available for such uses, though, during his lifetime, he would ask that it should not be so applied without his knowledge and verbal consent. But even in this there was to be no legal formality. He gave her his entire trust. And if he should die while this position continued, the money would remain under her control and disposition, to be used as she would suppose that he would desire.

To maintain the secrecy of the arrangement, he stipulated that she should render no accounts to him, nor communicate with him under whatever circumstances, either by letter or telephone. Periodically he would call upon her. Apart from such visits he wished her to act without consultation with him. He said, with some truth, that if they once allowed this rule to be broken, they would become lax and, in the end, the purpose he had in mind would be overset.

During the following years she had justified his confidence. Herself desiring no more than he said—to gain (on a spurious basis) a reputation for extreme philanthropy—she had maintained an almost absolute secrecy both in her relations with himself and in the benefactions which she bestowed.

With long intervals, he made calls upon her which were rarely of more than a few hours' duration. He found her accounts to be in order. He could congratulate himself upon a judgement of character which the event confirmed. From time to time he brought her fresh sums to be invested, for the same object, in securities which he suggested. He now had over one hundred thousand pounds placed in this way—money which no investigation, apart from her own voluntary statement, would trace to himself; and the possession of which, rather than its disappearance, would have been difficult for him to explain.

Should trouble arise, such as he had now seen to shadow uncertainly in a disturbed sky, he would have a large sum here which he had no doubt that she would retransfer to himself on such a pretext as would be easy to make, and a place of possible resort where no one would be likely to suspect him to be.

Martha Braddock was not a fool. She was a woman of somewhat more than average shrewdness. It is evidence of his able duplicity that he had successfully sustained the character which it had been necessary to assume—the more easily done because it was akin to that which he had made it his habit to play. As the years had passed she had found herself looking forward to these short and infrequent meetings with a warmer anticipation. She appreciated the largeness of his trust in her. She respected the generosity of his dispositions. She was appreciative of the opportunities of benefaction which had become hers through him. She observed with scrupulosity the condition of anonymity which he had imposed upon her. When she got one of the telephone messages which usually gave a day's notice of a projected visit, a pleasant excitement stirred.

On this occasion, when he had telephoned (not from his own home; he was too detailed in all his cautions for that) his purpose of coming next afternoon, and asked whether she could put him up without inconvenience for a night or perhaps two, she had readily agreed. She might be a little mystified as to why such a request should be made, but it was one to which there could be only one possible reply.

So it came to be that, when he had surveyed the dubious situation to which, in spite of all his cunning, he had been brought by the errors of his subordinates, assisted by sportive chance, he was able to conclude with the more comfortable reflection that Martha cooked a most excellent chop.

He saw no great cause for fear. He knew nothing yet of the Adam Street fire, which smouldered and steamed as he laid down his knife and fork on a well-cleared plate. But he had given all the orders that the position required. He had nothing more to do, let matters go how they might. He drew back, with habitual caution, to a place of safety from which to watch how events would move.

CHAPTER XXVII.

MR. MILDEW PLANS

MRS. BRADDOCK kept a spare bedroom for her occasional visitors, which, by the Victorian tradition to which she adhered, was the best that the house contained. This was placed at Mr. Mildew's disposal, in addition to which there were the two downstairs rooms, back and front, of which the smaller back one, soberly but sufficiently furnished, was used for meals, and the front, brighter and more modern in its appointments, was equally at his service. It was, indeed, here that his hostess was inclined to assume that he would prefer to be, but his own inclination, to which she had the good sense to defer, after the dictates of hospitable persuasion had been observed, was rather for the garden side of the house.

His quarters were less spacious than those from which he had come. They had less comprehensive amenities. He had leisure for thought. Leisure for reading also, which Mrs. Braddock's bookshelves in the lounge must do their best to provide. Besides that he must give some time to discussion of the investments which Mrs. Braddock controlled, and the distribution of the income they brought, these being the ostensible objects for which he had come, and leading up to a proposal for which he must be prepared, though he hoped that there might be no occasion for it.

But this hope suffered some declension as his hostess passed over to him, with natural comments, the late edition of the *Evening News*, displaying on its front page, with a luridity which did not exceed the event, an account of a "Great Fire in Whitechapel," with details of its escaping menagerie, the death of the proprietor of the destroyed premises, and cautiously worded hints of sinister criminal activities which the catastrophe had revealed, even if they had not been its originating cause. In the late news column there were further details of ultimate explanatory significance to the man who must read them with no change of countenance, while commenting in the casual manner which the occasion required. It gave the names of two who had been trapped in, and hardly escaped from the burning building.

Excusing himself to his hostess, he retired to his own room to consider the significances of what he had read.

Beal was dead. There was gain in that. There had been others there who could disclose much of the criminal activities which he controlled, but no one else, he believed, who could connect him therewith. But Catsgill was alive, and what he could say—might, indeed, already have said—joined to the evidence of Limbrook and that damnably competent girl, when added to what the police must have discovered now, might produce a sum much greater than a mere addition of its component parts. Considering this, he was conscious of a cold fear of approaching doom.

But he had courage of its own kind, and, as it reasserted its control, reason came plausibly to its support. He reminded himself that the whole trouble had arisen from the perversity of most improbable circumstance rather than any blunder of oversight or error which he could lay to his own door. There were grounds for confidence there. It was an occasion for him to use the coolness of judgement, the firmness of decision, which he knew himself to possess, to the overcoming of those who owed their advantage to lucky chance rather than abilities which were probably not theirs.

He supposed himself to have, at least, a brief leisure, a brief security, providing only that he did not disclose his location by any imprudent appearance or communication; and he had satisfaction in the thought that if, against probability, he should be discovered, there could be no presumption that he had been followed in guilty flight. He could show good reason for having come, and that he had done so many times before. He would be bold, in that event, in admission of his relations with Mrs. Braddock, even to disclosure of the wealth which was in her hands, and the ostensible purpose of its deposit. It would be consistent with his professed philanthropy, rather than the character which the police would prefer to show.

But he did not anticipate that necessity. Rather, he proposed to use the time which he believed to be his for observation of what developments there might be, and for making his retreat secure if it should appear to be a necessary prudence to flee.

He saw himself as equally in a position to avoid needless flight, or risk in remaining, if the police should be collecting material for his arrest.

He would have liked to telephone his own home to ascertain that there had been no further calls from the C.I.D. That would tell him much. If he should defer such a call until the latter part of the following day, it might be of decisive significance. And he could trust his butler's discreet intelligence. Without the clumsiness of direct enquiry he would certainly be told if there had been such callers. But he put the thought aside. He had never used Mrs. Braddock's telephone for such communication, or for calling any of his associates, even of an innocent kind. Risks should be *absolutely* barred. That was the rule by which he had established the isolation of his retreat, with a caution maintained during many years, and he would not jeopardize it now that the hour of its use might be upon him. The essential point was that he should *be*, not that he should have the satisfaction of knowing that he was, secure. Only one call would he make, which had become essential, and that, even if it were tapped—an extreme improbability to one who had no knowledge of Constable Hitchins' observant sagacity—would tell nothing, owing to the forethought with which he had planned against a danger he had not expected to have to face. He must speak to—he *must* see—Boyle.

But that call would not be made tonight. Nor tomorrow. Saturday morning would be the far better time. And meanwhile he must get Martha to retransfer the securities. With them back in his own satchel, there was nothing for which he would not be fully prepared, either to hold his ground or to flee. And he anticipated little difficulty with her.

He went downstairs, chatted for a few minutes, pleaded a headache and an hour which was becoming late, and returned to his own room. He had arranged that the next day should be spent in a review of the benefactions which had been made possible by his generosity, and that this should lead to the recovered control of the fortune which he designed. The ashes of Maurice Beal's emporium still smouldered in Whitechapel. Its proprietor lay dead in the public mortuary. But Cornelius Mildew slept well.

CHAPTER XXVIII.

MR. MILDEW DOES WHAT HE INTENDS

FRIDAY, during which Inspector Cauldron and Billie wrestled with Mr. Belfrey, Eustace Limbrook drafted advertisements of his professional qualifications for *The Times* and the *Daily Telegraph*, while finding the eulogies of the Press inadequate consolation for his temporarily crippled feet, and Miss Brell digested a polite message from Scotland Yard informing her that her help was no longer needed, was, for Mr. Mildew, a quiet, pleasant, successful day.

He was living more simply than he was accustomed to do in his own comparatively palatial home. But there was no lack of essential comforts in Mrs. Braddock's more restricted residence. Her cooking was good, her single maid of a well-trained efficiency.

Seated beside her at breakfast, disposing of excellent coffee and a dish of eggs and bacon which his own cook could not have bettered, he made the proposal which he had shaped during the night.

"It is likely," he said, "that I may have occasion to go abroad for a long—indeed, for an indefinite—period. It is for that reason that I desired to meet you at somewhat greater leisure than we have found sufficient on other occasions."

A slight pause followed this opening, and then Mrs. Braddock replied equably: "In that case you would probably prefer to make some different arrangements about the shares?"

Both pleased and surprised to have his purpose so quickly guessed and so quietly met, he yet protested: "My dear Mrs. Braddock! As though such a thought should have crossed my mind! My confidence in you is too absolute to be strained by any difficulty of communication. Surely we know each other too well for such a thought to arise between us...! And yet there is a sense in which you are right, though for a reason which you might not think, and in a way which will show how unshaken my trust remains.

"It may not have interested you to watch the fluctuations of the investment market, and you may be unaware that we appear to be on the threshold of one of those periods of depression which alternate with more prosperous times. At such periods heavy losses may fall upon those who do not watch the signs of a changing sky.

"Even should I leave you the most detailed instructions regarding the circumstances under which you should realize or reinvest, they might be difficult to follow, and would impose upon you an anxious responsibility.

"What I propose is that the stocks shall be placed under the control of my own brokers, in whose discretion I have entire confidence, with power to deal with them at their discretion, and that arrangements should be made with the bankers with whom they will be lodged to advance a sum of fifty thousand pounds upon them, which will be deposited in your name, so that you can not only use the interest, but draw upon the principal at your discretion if you should think well to do so, as the objects in which we are interested may require.

"I know already that you will have provided against the possibility that you may predecease me: you can rely upon the contrary—and more probable—event placing the whole original sum under your undivided control."

Mrs. Braddock said bluntly: "I think you trust me too far."

"That," Mr. Mildew replied with more sincerity than he had spoken before, "is what it would not be easy to do."

Having said this, he turned the conversation to other topics, and when, later in the day, he proposed that she should get out the securities, which lay in a small safe installed at his cost in the wall of the dining-room, and then produced, and filled in with the ease of familiarity, the undated transfer forms which his plan required, was it likely that she would object to sign them? That there must be an interval between her losing control of the securities and being put in possession of the fund which was to replace them was not a point which she would have been likely to raise, even had she the claim of more substantial ownership. Under the actual circumstances, having raised no objection to the scheme itself, it would have been an impossible attitude to adopt. Indeed, had he asked straightforwardly for the return of the wealth he had entrusted to her, on such a plea as that of financial reverses, it is most improbable that she would have demurred.

But to take so simple a course would have been contrary to his own character, and open to the valid objection that, if arrest and enquiry should follow, it would have supplied the presumption that he had been preparing for secret flight, without the specious though inadequate explanation that he would now have to offer.

As it was, he was able to retire that night with the satisfaction of having found far-sighted precautions equal to the occasion against which they had been designed.

He believed himself to be securely hidden from the observations of the police. He knew himself to be in clear control of a fortune of not less than one hundred thousand pounds, which it would be very difficult—perhaps impossible—to trace to his possession, and which he should be able to realize at leisure, if the perversity of circumstance should separate him from the wealth that was in his own name.

But he was still hopeful that such necessity would not arise. The very fact that his forethought had prepared him so thoroughly to deal with the emergency increased his confidence that he could control it now.

But that was a matter on which decision must be left to the next day. Tomorrow morning he would summon Boyle, and when he had his report he would be better able to judge.

With little prescience, for all his sagacity and all his cunning, of what the events of the next day would be, and least of all of the direction from which his most deadly danger would come, he retired with some cause to congratulate himself on a successful day; and once again he slept well.

CHAPTER XXIX.

MR. MILDEW COMPLETES HIS PLANS

"I WONDER," Mr. Mildew said casually, "whether I might trespass upon your kindness to telephone a short message for me when breakfast is over. It is a business communication of some importance—that is, it is important that it should be conveyed with accuracy—but it is a matter on which I do not wish to be drawn into conversation, as would be probable if I should speak myself."

This was on Saturday morning. Mrs. Braddock, who was in the act of pouring him a second cup of coffee, glanced up from the urn as she answered: "Yes, of course…. But perhaps, if it's so important to be exact, you'd better write it down."

That had been his intention. He said: "Well, as you like." He drew out a small notebook, wrote a few lines in a small, neat, spidery script, tore it out, and passed it to her. She read:

Terminus 6674.

Will Mr. Younger please make up the book to the date agreed, and send it to number six.

"Yes," she said, "I don't think I need make any mistake about that." She folded the little slip and pushed it under the side of her plate.

He said: "I feel I must not trespass on your hospitality further. If it would be convenient for me to stay until the early evening? Perhaps until about six?"

"You know you are welcome to stay as long as you please. It has been a pleasure to have you. But I am afraid it must have been rather dull for you."

She spoke with a simple sincerity, not as one expecting the obvious disclaimer, giving him a direct glance from grey-blue eyes that were still bright and clear, though many wrinkles were round them now. He answered, with the facile, convincing courtesy that he was practised to use: "Indeed, no! It has been a most pleasant and restful time."

The telephone was an old-fashioned wall instrument in the hall. He remained seated at the breakfast table at the conclusion of the meal after she had risen to make the promised call. Through the half-open door he heard her give the message with careful correctness. Almost immediately she hung up. He judged that there had been no hitch there.

She came back to say: "Mr. Younger didn't seem to want to speak to you. He said it should have attention at once."

Mr. Mildew was precise. "That was just what he said? You are sure that was the word he used?"

Mrs. Braddock was sure. He said: "Then I can put that from my mind. Younger is a most reliable man."

He glanced at a marble clock that ticked on the mantelpiece with slow sedateness. It was a quarter past nine. He said: "I thought to have mentioned that I may have a friend calling to see me this afternoon. It won't be before one, or a quarter past. It might be later. I hope it won't be inconvenient for me to see him alone? I could take him upstairs if—"

"No, of course not. I'll tell the girl to show him into the front room. You can be alone there as long as you like. Or perhaps he might be here for lunch?"

No, Mr. Mildew thought not. He would be sure to have had lunch before calling.

He went up to his own room. He had matters of which to think. But he was not greatly concerned. Things were going smoothly and as he meant them to do.

He had no suspicion that the telephone conversation which had just taken place was already the subject of a note upon Superintendent Backwash's desk. But if he had he would have said, with truth, that there could be small danger in that. The police could find that it had been received at a political club in the Gray's Inn Road. They might be puzzled. But it was of an apparent innocence, and it would be a clue that their enquiries would never catch.

It was, in fact, a code summons to the man who, next to, and more actively than himself, was in control of the operations of the gang. A man of such family and connections that the police were most unlikely to suspect him of criminal courses. One who, on three occasions, had actually been able to use influence which had turned enquiry aside when it had been too closely upon the track of important though subordinate members. One who was as able, energetic, and ruthless in executing as was Mildew in issuing the punitive orders which discipline would at times require.

The man who received the message would not send it forward upon his own telephone. Within two minutes of its receipt, a youth, whistling carelessly, would stroll along the Grey's Inn Road, enter a call-box, and telephone a different message, of equally innocent sound, to the chambers of the Hon. Peter Boyle, and it would require a supernatural diligence and acuteness on the part of the C.I.D. to become aware of the two messages and connect them in any way.

When Boyle should receive the message he would refer to a list of addresses among his papers and select that which was indicated by the message. "Number six" was the one to which, putting whatever else aside, he was to go four hours after the call had been received, or as soon after as any delay in its delivery or his own movements might allow. The list of addresses included all which, at a moment of crisis, Mildew might desire to use for such a meeting. They were not written out plainly, but cryptically confused and altered, so that, even if the list should fall into hostile hands, it would be no more than a misleading guide. Precautions were taken very thoroughly in the Mildew Gang, and Peter Boyle, nodding casually before his shaving glass (for he was a man who rose late) as his secretary gave him a most innocent-sounding message which had just come for him over the phone, resolved that there should be no exception on this occasion. He felt a confidence which was not entirely correct that however many members of the gang, high or low, might require elimination due to those who had blundered or fallen under the suspicion of the police, no one now suspected him.

CHAPTER XXX.

PRELUDE TO BATTLE

IT was about twenty to twelve when Billie rang the bell at 9, Blake Terrace, and the maid opened the door. She had given the push a short and somewhat diffident pressure, as a charity canvasser surely should, and Mr. Mildew, reading in the back room, was undisturbed. At intervals during the morning it was inevitable that tradesmen should ring, and the maid would be heard to come and go along the narrow hall, but the sounds had no importance to him. He was securely hidden. His plans were complete. His mind at ease. When Boyle should come he would receive his report, and his instructions to him might vary according to its nature, as might his own course of action, but he felt that there would be no contingency for which he was not fully prepared.

He had glanced over two morning papers without discovering any reference to himself (which he scarcely feared) or to the disclosures which had followed the Adam Street catastrophe. Probably the police had learned nothing on which they could proceed against him or his organization further, and would be content with the spectacular triumph they had obtained.

Lunch had been arranged for twelve-thirty, to assure that it would be over before the coming of Mr. Mildew's expected visitor. Now he was occupying his time in reading *Sense and Sensibility*, which he had found the day before, in three-volume form, in the bookcase in the front room. He appreciated its particularity, and was near the end of the second volume as a bell rang which he did not heed.

Billie asked: "Is Mrs. Braddock at home? I should like to see her for a few minutes."

The maid, not asking her to step in, answered hesitatingly: "Yes. What name, please?"

She knew that her mistress was engaged in the kitchen, being particular in the preparation of the lunch which her guest must share. And the young lady, however pleasant she might look, was a stranger to one who thought she knew all Mrs. Braddock's friends; and it was not an hour at which any visitors were accustomed to call.

Billie had decided to avoid giving her name, if possible, but to do so rather than use a false one, which would be futile should she be recognized by any of the Mildew Gang, and needless if she were not.

"Miss Wingrove. She won't know the name. But you might say that I shan't keep her more than a few minutes."

But the girl still did not move. "What business shall I say, miss?"

It was a second question she had wished to avoid. Even a lady of philanthropic reputation might not consent to see every canvasser who called at the door. But there might be no wisdom in declining to answer. "I've called," she said, "on behalf of the Chislehurst Women's and Children's Hospital," and as she said it, and the girl withdrew from the door, she knew that she had got something wrong with the name, which was in her bag and should have been equally in her mind; but was there any need for worry in that?

She was far more concerned lest she should be rebuffed at the door, and beyond that she had the doubt of how she could develop the interview, if she should gain it, to the end she sought.

She would beg for a subscription. It would be given or denied. Then she would be led back to the door. What gain would there be? Well, perhaps some. She would be able to form a personal opinion of Mrs. Braddock. Perhaps to observe something which would be relevant in other was. Only why did these enterprises seem so much more hopeful at a distant view than when you stood at the door?

Yet, she reminded herself, she had not failed at the Adam Street shop, or the highly polished counter of the inspector of taxes—nor, before that, once when she had called with Eustace at Mr. Mildew's imposing home, and more perilously at an upstairs room at the Reader's Grill.

Now she needed her wits and eyes not for introspection but instant use.... "Will you come in, miss?" the girl was saying, at a door which was opened more widely than it had been before.

Billie was led into the front room, asked to take a chair, and left for some minutes to her own reflections.

She surveyed her surroundings with alert eyes, but could observe nothing inconsistent with the personality which Mrs. Braddock showed to the world. If she could claim to have learned anything, it was no more than that what might be a false aspect did not finish at the front door. But she could see no evidence of Mr. Mildew's or any other masculine presence. Nothing that did not support the quiet, comfortable, rather staid respectability of Mrs. Braddock's long-established reputation. Her eyes searched for the "clue" which should have been there by all the canons of the detective's art; but, if there were any such, it was not for her. She even noticed that there was a slight gap in the bookshelves between the first and third volumes of *Sense and Sensibility*, though she could not possibly realize its importance, or that Mr. Mildew was even then closing the missing volume, thinking of fetching the one that followed, and then sitting unmoved as his mind wandered back over the events of recent weeks, and settled upon the memory of a young woman who, he saw with malignant clarity, had been, after the caprice of circumstance, more directly responsible even than Eustace Limbrook for the peril which was around him now. Well, Boyle should have the instructions regarding her which her persistence deserved. Beal was dead. For his smuggling uses it was a loss which would be hard to replace. But for deeds of secret violence others could be found who would be equal to him. It was a matter on which Boyle would be most unlikely to fail.

Mr. Mildew's reflections continued in uninterrupted leisure, but Billie's were broken abruptly by the entrance, of Mrs. Braddock, who said, with characteristic directness, as her visitor rose: "Do sit down. I understand you've called about the Chislehurst Hospital?"

Billie looked at the speaker as she settled herself in her own chair, and knew that she had learned much, though it might be of a negative order. "I'm no good at this job," she thought, "if this woman knows anything about criminal gangs beyond what she may read in the *Evening News*." She reminded herself that Inspector Cauldron had told her that there are no criminal types, and she knew that Mr. Mildew himself—but it was more than that. She was instinctively, certainly convinced that she was faced by one who was utterly unconcerned as to what she herself might be, or whether she could have any object she did not show; one who had a mind at ease from any anxiety more serious than that of how soon she might be free to inspect the state of a cooking joint.

As she thought thus she became as eloquent upon the Chislehurst Hospital's need of a new wing as her very limited knowledge and preoccupation of mind allowed, but the latter handicap may have been too great, for Mrs. Braddock asked with a directness of doubt which the quietly modulated voice did not entirely conceal: "Have you been collecting long?"

Billie realized that while her own mind had been occupied in exonerating the older woman, that of Mrs. Braddock had been directed upon herself toward a contrary verdict. Her instinct of combat roused itself to the challenge. A laughing candour was in her eyes as she replied: "No, I can't say I have. But how did you spot that?"

"I hear a good many appeals. You can tell when they've been said many times before."

"And mine sounds like the first time?"

"Yes, or the time before that."

Mrs. Braddock's smile now met that of her visitor without reserve, the frankness of Billie's admission having dismissed that which had been no more than a puzzled doubt.

"I hope," Billie went on, "you won't refuse me because of that?"

"Certainly not for that reason. I don't know that I shall refuse you at all. It was a cause to which I was already thinking of sending a small donation. But it would have been direct to Mr. Kemp. Will it make any difference if I give it to you...? You know Mr. Kemp, of course?"

Billie saw that she was in deeper waters than those in which she had expected to wade. She had made unfortunate choice of this Chislehurst Hospital because its needs had been the subject of a long advertisement in a morning paper—an advertisement which was now in her bag. Could she be expected to guess that Mrs. Braddock would have personal acquaintances on its board or staff? Well, perhaps she should. It was at least a possibility in approaching one who had a reputation, however modestly concealed, for opening her cheque book in such directions.

"No," she said, answering the last question first with the same frankness as before, "I can't say I do." And then, seeing the purport of the first, quick wit taking the place of a knowledge which was not hers: "Yes, it will be all the same. You can send it direct if you like. I'm not charging them a commission, if you mean that."

Mrs. Braddock rose. She went to her desk and drew a cheque-book from a side drawer. She knew that most canvassers are remunerated in one form or another. She knew that this charge upon charitable donations varies from a commission which scarcely keeps the collectors alive to a rake-off of the bulk of the money that is received. It was hard to say where that which was legitimate ended and fraud began; but she preferred to make her donations direct, so that such deductions should not occur.

Her present caller, though puzzling to her shrewd and experienced eyes, did not look to be one of the baser sort, and she was inclined to believe the assurance that she had received. But she was cautious in method still. "I am going to give you ten pounds. Would you like the cheque to be made out to yourself?"

It was a test question, which was satisfactorily met. "Oh no, of course not. You'd better cross it to the hospital."

"You'd better give me the name exactly."

"It's—the Chislehurst Women's and Children's Hospital. That's sufficiently exact, anyhow. I don't suppose there are two."

"No-o. But I like to be accurate. Isn't there the word *District* in it...? Haven't you any literature with you?"

Billie hesitated. Should she open her bag and refer to the advertisement, which would surely give the information required? It would be a poor armoury for a collector to carry. Or should she take the bolder course which was already half-formed in her mind as she had talked, and tell Mrs. Braddock frankly why she had come, and the suspicion under which the house, perhaps by an absolute error of Constable Hitchins, lay?

But as she paused Mrs. Braddock laid down her pen. "Miss— Miss Wingrove," she asked, "will you tell me why you are here?"

"I am collecting for the Chislehurst Hospital."

"Yes. So I understand. I asked you why you are doing that.... You should know—I suppose you do—that there are police restrictions on collecting for charitable objects within the metropolitan area."

"I don't think I need worry about that." Billie smiled confidently, but the gravity of Mrs. Braddock's face did not change.

"But perhaps you should. It is a matter on which ignorance is not easily accepted as an excuse. You mustn't please think that I am suggesting anything wrong if I ask you to show me whatever authorization you have with you."

"I think perhaps I'd better tell you the whole tale."

"Yes. I think you had." Billie saw distance, but no hostility, in the glance she met. She had no fear of the police, and some confidence that there was wisdom in a candid statement of the suspicions which had surrounded the house with unsuspected watchers; but, most inopportunely for her, it was at that moment that Mr. Mildew entered the room.

CHAPTER XXXI.

A SUDDEN BATTLE OF WITS

MR. MILDEW had a book in his hand. He said: "Excuse me. I didn't know you had a visitor. If I may just exchange...."—and then he saw who that visitor was.

Billie had less reason to be surprised, and a full second of extra time in which to adjust her mind to the encounter which she saw at once must be fought without mercy on either side. She could not tell what might be the standing of her opponent in the house, or what support he might have, but to obtain that of Mrs. Braddock against him must be her immediate object. Equally, and almost as instantly, Mr. Mildew saw that to discredit her, and anything she might already have said, must be his. It was a battle of wits in which neither side had time for preparation nor complete knowledge of where the antagonist's weakness lay. Mrs. Braddock, with no faintest perception of what it meant, was yet conscious, in that first moment of recognition, that they had met before and were not friends. The knowledge naturally prejudiced her against the one who was strange to her.

She said: "Mr. Mildew, perhaps you'll stay a moment, if you don't mind. This young lady has called upon me for a subscription to the Chislehurst Hospital. She was just going to tell me how she came to take up the work and what her credentials are."

The words were not unpleasantly said. Billie realized that she was not condemned in advance. Mrs. Braddock would give a fair, even a friendly, hearing to whatever she might have to say. But she was yet called on for her defence. It was she who was in the dock, and to reverse the position, even though Mrs. Braddock should have no sympathy with, or know ledge of Mr. Mildew's criminal activities, might be no easy matter. Indeed, the more of innocent confidence there was the harder it might be.

"I was just going to—" Billie began.

Mr. Mildew spoke at the same time. "Miss Wingrove and I have met before. I didn't know she was interested in hospitals. I should say she knows more about selling dope."

The audacity of the accusation roused his opponent to an equally frontal attack. "Yes," she said, "so I do. At least, I know who the police are anxious to get."

"Miss Wingrove," Mr. Mildew said coolly, without taking notice of this retort, "called upon me recently in company with a man who admitted that he had considered an offer to peddle dope. His excuse was impecuniosity. I had to tell him that our acquaintance, such as it was, could not continue. Miss Wingrove was with him, and their relations appeared to be of a particularly friendly character. I could not observe that she was repelled by the confession he made, but she may have seen reason to change her occupation since."

Billie said: "I don't see what good you can do for yourself by talking such utter rot. You know the whole trouble was that you tried to get Eustace to help you in smuggling dope, and he told the police."

"Miss Wingrove," Mrs. Braddock interrupted these exchanges to say, "you may honestly believe that for all I know; but I can assure you that it is utter nonsense. Will you please keep to the point, and let me see your credentials as a collector for the Chislehurst Hospital?"

Billie declined to be diverted from an attack which was the sole defence she had. "Mrs. Braddock," she said, "I suppose you've read about the Adam Street."

"Yes, I have. But I fail to see how it can have anything to do with the explanation for which I ask."

"Well, it has. It's what I was just going to tell you when Mr. Mildew came in. I was the girl who nearly got killed there. You may remember reading the name."

"Still I don't see—"

"But Mr. Mildew does. You might ring up the police, and—"

"That," Mr. Mildew said, "was just what I was proposing to do."

"I wish you'd do it yourself, Mrs. Braddock, please. If you'd ask for Superintendent Backwash, and say—"

"I think," Mr. Mildew interrupted, "that you had better leave this to me. I wish this young woman no harm, but it seems evident that she has some very undesirable associates, and that she is unable to produce a proper authority for the work in which she is engaged.

It appears to be a matter with which the police should deal, and they will give her every opportunity of explaining what she's been doing here."

"Considering that they know already—"

"If you are already known to the police, they will be the more easily able to judge of the innocence of what you are doing now."

"Yes, they certainly will. You can ring up either Superintendent Backwash or Inspector Cauldron at Scotland Yard—" But that, as she had feared, was not what he intended to do.

"I am afraid," he said, "that I cannot allow you to dictate to me in that manner. It is a matter—in the first instance at least—for the local police. Whether your case should prove to be of sufficient importance to justify a reference to higher officials must be for them to decide."

"There might be no harm—" Mrs. Braddock suggested doubtfully.

"Perhaps not. But there would be delay, and I am sure you will wish us to be relieved of this young woman's presence as quickly as possible. Besides, it would make me look rather a fool."

Mr. Mildew looked at his watch as he spoke, and stepped quickly into the hall. Billie saw the subtlety of her opponent's action, though she could not know the urgency of his desire to get her out of the house before another caller should be at the door.

She saw that, as he had done at moments of crisis before, he was adopting an attitude which might afterwards be argued to be one which only innocence would prefer. She saw also that, while she had nothing ultimately to fear, the immediate result of communicating with the local police station might be awkward for her. Or it might not. It would depend upon how much they already knew. Probably, in view of the watch which was being kept on the house, enough to prevent any inconvenience to her. That was where, in ignorance of the true position, he might overreach himself.

But though she was in no fear, she was in some confusion of mind as to how far she should be content with what she had done, as she heard his voice in the hall: "Yes. The Trench Street station will do.... Yes, I should like to speak to...any responsible officer."

She saw that she had at least unearthed the man the police sought. There could be no further doubt of his presence there, no reason to hesitate to enter or search the house, if a warrant had been issued for his arrest. Indeed, that would hardly be necessary; he was opening the door to them, so to speak, with his own hands. Well, she must wait to see what would follow. But meanwhile she had a curiously strong desire to justify herself to the woman who was watching her now with shrewdly speculative but not unfriendly eyes.

Listening with one ear to Mr. Mildew's voice in the hall with the other she heard Mrs. Braddock say: "I'm very sorry, Miss Wingrove, to have to take this course, and I hope you'll be able to put matters right with the police. But illicit collecting of this kind does harm in so many ways—"

"Oh, I'm not troubling about the police! They know more about my being here than Mr. Mildew's telling them now. But please do believe that I'm not an illicit canvasser. Or perhaps I am, but what I mean is, if you'd given a cheque it would have gone to the hospital. There'd have been nothing wrong about that. But I really came to find out whether Mr. Mildew were hiding here, which the police were anxious to know."

Mrs. Braddock said dryly: "Well, he doesn't seem to mind that." She was not credulous of the accusations she had heard, which seemed absurd in themselves, and such as a loyal friendship should decline to heed; but she was shrewd enough to perceive that the truth might be something different from that which she had supposed.

Billie answered: "You mayn't believe me now. Perhaps it isn't natural that you should. But you'll soon know.... But if you've listened you may have noticed he's not mentioned his own name. He's only spoken for you."

So it had been, though that might also be explicable to any but a suspicious mind. It was Mrs. Braddock upon whom Billie had called. Presumably it was her matter and her complaint.

Mr. Mildew's emphasis had been upon the question of time. Inspector Craig had said: "Don't let her go. You must keep her somehow till I get round." To which Mr. Mildew had replied: "How is Mrs. Braddock to do that?" Inspector Craig said he'd be round himself in about four minutes. Mr. Mildew said Mrs. Braddock would be very glad if he would.

Hanging up the receiver, he looked at his watch again. The police station was only two streets away. Probably the inspector would be as good as his word. Calculating coolly, he thought that there would be time enough. Time to get her out of the house before Boyle should come. He did not want too much time. He saw that, under whatever circumstances Billie had really come to the house, however she had traced him there, and however much or little the police might already know, she would be sure to disclose his presence now in her own defence. He could not tell what the consequences might be, but as a secret retreat the use of the house was done.

He would have stopped Boyle if he could, but it was too late for that. Yet, if he could keep his nerve, all might still be well. There might even be time for lunch, after the police had taken her away and before Boyle should come. He would prefer not to miss that.

He said as he re-entered the room: "The police will be here in about a couple of minutes. If I can do anything further for you, Martha, you won't hesitate to call on me. But I think it will be better if I am not present when you make the charge, especially as Miss Wingrove appears to think that I am unfriendly to her. Actually, I have no such feeling, but she has a most dangerous, reckless tongue. Perhaps you can persuade her, before the inspector gets here, of the wisdom of keeping to the point if she's got any explanation to give."

Billie said: "I think you live in lies till you sometimes almost deceive yourself."

Mr. Mildew took no notice of that. He went back to the room in which the lunch was being laid, forgetting to take the book for which he had come. *Sense and Sensibility* was one which he was not destined to finish, unless it penetrate to another world.

He left the door slightly open, being interested to hear what might occur, which proved to be satisfactory to him.

He heard that Billie, her request to ring up Scotland Yard put curtly aside, was required to go round to the police station to be formally charged. He heard her repeated protest, "I don't care what you charge me with, if you let Inspector Cauldron know," and the reply that that would be for the superintendent to say.

Well, she might succeed in getting word to Scotland Yard. He supposed she very soon would. They wouldn't detain her without bail and refuse her permission to communicate with her friends. He knew enough about police procedure to be sure of that. But it did not follow that it would make any trouble—certainly not any immediate trouble—for him. Nor would it look well for him to go too promptly. Fortunately he had already told Martha that he would leave in the afternoon. The talk with Boyle needn't keep him long.... He sat down to a loin of pork, expertly cooked. He liked kidney. He praised the sauce He had had many more elaborate meals, but few that he had enjoyed more.

CHAPTER XXXII.

He Called and He Went Away

INSPECTOR CRAIG, a somewhat stiff official member of the force, conducted his prisoner into the car which had brought him to Blake Terrace, and as the vehicle moved from the pavement, he leaned back and his manner changed. "I suppose I need not tell you, Miss Wingrove, that you are not really under arrest. Inspector Cauldron is waiting at the Trench Street station to see you."

"I couldn't quite make it out," Billie replied. "But I didn't think I should be under arrest long."

She spoke gaily, in reaction from an experience which she had not liked, however confident of ultimate exculpation she may have been; but her companion was stolid in his reply: "It was a good thing that we knew what you were."

Whatever he may have known, he showed no curiosity as to what her experiences had been, or even whether it were Mildew's voice which had summoned him to the arrest. In fact, he spoke no further words until he arrived at the Trench Street station. Billie concluded that he was a dull stick, which was somewhat unfair to a zealous and conscientious officer, but she wasted little thought upon him, having more engaging matters upon her mind.

She greeted Inspector Cauldron with a kinder glance than he often got from her direction, having made a correct guess that it was consideration for her safety which had brought him there, and it being a solicitude which she approved.

Unlike Inspector Craig, he was urgent for explicit details of her experiences, and was soon telephoning them to Superintendent Backwash, with whom he agreed that Mildew's action was a further evidence of the formidable subtlety of their opponent's methods, and the care that would be needed to catch him in a net that he could not break. But, be that as it might, it appeared that the hour of hesi-

155

tation was past. The Home Secretary himself had asked for a full digest of the evidence which was in the hands of the Yard, and had endorsed the Commissioner's opinion that it was enough—that, in any case, they had gone too far to draw back.

Mildew was to be followed whenever he should leave the house, and arrested whether he should return to his own home or (as was hoped) go to some other address as little suspected as that of Mrs. Braddock had been. For it was still evident that there must be others of a more actively executive capacity controlling the operations of the gang of whose identities they had no knowledge, apart from the meagre details, and the two most improbable names that the injured Catsgill could supply.

The house was now watched more closely than before, both at front and back, and the first hour brought a report that a taxi had driven up to the door and a man had entered. There was no furtiveness about this proceeding, the taxi waiting at the kerb. But when Inspector Cauldron heard of it he gave orders at once that the driver should be spoken to, if possible on the other side of the vehicle, and so that the action should be unobserved from the house, and instructed to notice his passenger with care, so that he could identify him with certainty if he should be called on to do so, and that he should also take a note of the address to which he should convey him.

It was an obvious precaution to take, and had it been done, it might have had consequences for the Hon. Peter Boyle which would have been unpleasant for him, but, in fact, it was an abortive order. The officer who had been detailed to execute it reported that he had been about thirty seconds too late. He had only been able to watch the vehicle moving away.

Inspector Cauldron spoke to the sergeant who was in charge of the watch which was kept upon the front of the house.

"Couldn't you," he asked, "have taken so obvious a precaution without orders from me? And why wasn't the taxi followed? Don't you realize that, whoever came, it may have been Mildew who got away?"

The young officer; flustered but firm, said that he knew it was not. It was a man of quite different build who had entered and left the house. He could swear to that. Could he identify him? No, he wouldn't say that. He hadn't had a near enough view. But he had the number of the taxi. It would be easy to question the driver. The information might not be difficult to obtain.

As to that, the driver was found in the next hour, but he had little useful information to give. His passenger had been picked up in Leicester Square. He had got in as another fare had alighted outside the Odeon Picture House. After the call at Blake Terrace he had driven him to the Waldorf and been paid off there. Could he identify him? No, he wouldn't say that he could. Not old. Not so young for that matter. Had a husky voice and coughed more than a bit. Rather a toff, if they asked him.

There was not much use in that, especially as the husky voice and the coughs were parts of a deliberate well-studied disguise which the Hon. Peter used for such occasions, of a finer and safer kind than those that paint and hair can provide...

Inspector Cauldron listened to the sergeant's defence and recognized that, if there were blame, he might fairly take a share for himself, for he should have given more explicit orders against the possibilities of such an event. But what he would have said will never be known, for he was interrupted to take a call from No. 9, Blake Terrace, whose occupants were appealing once more for the assistance of the police.

CHAPTER XXXIII.

"LE ROI EST MORT: VIVE LE ROI"

THE HON. Peter Boyle arrived punctually at Blake Terrace, and frowned at that which he saw. He was younger than Cornelius Mildew, of sharper speech and brisker manner, but it would be hard to say which was the more cunning, more specious, or less scrupulous man.

They were alike in determining that, though their incomes might be derived from illegal practices and defended by violent crimes, they would act with such discreet and distant obliquities as would keep them clear from the iron reach of the law. Now Boyle looked at a type of house such as he would be unlikely to visit in a social way, and frowned at what he regarded as an indiscretion of choice on the part of a colleague on whose cautious cunning even his arrogant self-assurance had become accustomed to lean. Yet there might be reasons he did not know.

He did know that the secrecy of their organization was gravely threatened, and that they had already lost men, Maurice Beal in particular, who would be hard to replace. More surprising, he knew that Mildew himself was more nearly involved than he had supposed he would ever be. He had expected this summons to come, but he had supposed that the place of meeting would be of less incongruous and therefore less conspicuous choice. But he had not known his chief to blunder in such matters—he had not known him to blunder at all till now—and it was a rendezvous which he could not change.

He had the fare ready, with a liberal though not excessive tip, as the car slowed down at the kerb. He did not look directly at the driver, for he had a theory that men remember one another better if their eyes meet; but he added a separate half-crown as he said: "If you like to wait ten or twenty minutes, I shall most likely want you again. I shan't keep you longer than that." He ran up the steps, glanced back at a driver who was not looking at him, and left and right at a road which showed no life beyond that of an old woman moving away on its further side.

The maid admitted him when he enquired for Mr. Mildew, without asking his name, and showed him at once into the front room, where that gentleman joined him a moment later.

"In a bit of a mess, aren't you?" Boyle asked abruptly, without offering his hand, which Mr. Mildew did not appear to expect, but there was emphasis on the plural pronoun when he replied: "We have had a nasty shaking up, but I don't see why it should go farther than it already has."

"Well, I'm here to know what it is and what you wish me to do."

"The mischief comes from the man Limbrook. I needn't explain who he is. You'll have seen enough about him in the press. It was the sort of thing which no one could foresee. He'll have to be got rid of somehow, and I must leave that to you. I can't tell whether the police have any suspicions of me—they can't have anything worse than that—but I shall stand back for a few weeks and leave everything in your hands. The closer they watch me the better I shall be pleased, and when they've made up their minds that they're barking under the wrong tree you'll hear from me again."

"I suppose you know they've been turning your house upside down?"

Mr. Mildew heard this news with an exclamation he could not repress. It showed his danger to be greater than he had hoped, if not than he had feared it to be. And the idea was distasteful in itself to one of a fastidious mind. But he controlled himself quickly. Boyle was a colleague, but not therefore a friend. He said easily: "Well, they'll draw a blank there. They'll have had their first disappointment by now."

Peter Boyle said nothing to that. The significant point to him was that Mildew had not been aware of what was happening. Was he really losing his grip? There might be danger in that—danger for Peter Boyle from the only direction from which it would be possible for it to come.

It was a contingency which he had considered and for which he had prepared, before the summons of the morning had been received. But he had come with an open mind. And he listened carefully now to the further instructions that Mildew was giving, instructions and information concisely worded, and dealing only with vital matters of organization, discipline and distribution, for Mildew had always avoided the details which his predecessor had pursued to his own disaster. He ended by reverting to the trouble which was driving him, if not to flight, to retirement now. Catsgill, like Limbrook, must be dealt with, but with a particular discretion, in view of what had happened before, and the fact that he was under the watchful protection of the police. He could trust Boyle for that. But his final emphasis was on the necessity for eliminating Billie Wingrove, apart from which he said that no one in the gang, including themselves, would ever be able to feel secure. He said she had a genius for finding out what wasn't meant for her—or it might be the devil's luck—but it had got to be stopped—would have been stopped before now if Bolton hadn't been a blundering fool, and even Maurice Beal, though he'd been sharp enough to guess who she was, must have let himself be outwitted, so that it was he who was a dead man.

Boyle said: "I shouldn't worry about that. I think I know those who'll be equal to settling her." He considered how quiet the house was, how short a distance it was to the front door, how deserted the road had been, how soon the waiting taxi would be moving away. He repeated: "I don't think you need trouble any more about her. You've got a nearer trouble than that now."

He fired from his jacket pocket—twice, and the body of Cornelius Mildew sagged limply in his chair.

Boyle rose without loss of time and without haste. "Well," he muttered, "I'll say that was neatly done."

He drew the weapon from his pocket, removing the silencer, wiped it carefully, and placed it where it would have lain had it fallen from the hand of a dying man.

He saw a danger removed and himself the unchallenged head of a gang of which, in fact, he was already in active control. He went quietly to the hall, let himself out, and got into the waiting taxi.

CHAPTER XXXIV.

To End Is to Begin

BILLIE opened amazed eyes. "You mean," she asked, "that you know he did it, and won't do anything?"

"I mean," Inspector Cauldron answered, "that we sometimes know things that we can't prove; and it's silly to alarm a man that you're not ready to put where he ought to be."

"If everyone had as many reasons for doing nothing as I've heard in the last three months from the C.I.D.—"

"There might be fewer mistakes made. I don't suppose you were going to say that. But when you've been with us a bit longer, Miss Wingrove, you'll know that there are things that we can't afford. The public—"

"I know all that by heart. But you needn't be so formal. It can be Billie to you. We're brother officers now, even if you do think me a fool."

Watching the effect of her words, Billie was half disposed to regret the offer of familiarity which she had made. Inspector Cauldron (she told herself) was a nice boy. But anyone stupider in his dealings with girls it would be hard to find. In fact, he didn't know how to begin, and she wasn't going to show any hurry in running after him. Still, it was rather fun to see how he felt, and that he didn't know how to go ahead. It was rather comic in a man who aimed to be a star of the C.I.D.

"You know," he said, "I don't think you are a fool." She noticed that he did not avail himself of the privilege he had been offered, though he did not call her Miss Wingrove again. He went on: "We think you're one of the brightest we've ever had, and you ought to be safer as one of us than when you were just one of the public who gave us a helping hand. There aren't many who'll risk attacking one of the force."

"No. I remember Mr. Catsgill saying something like that, though he put it in a different way. He seemed to think it was a matter on which the public get what Americans would call a raw deal. But I'm not one who ought to complain.... But I don't see that Eustace or I have got much to worry about now that Mildew's dead."

"I hope you're right about that. But I don't think it's a very good reason to give. It wasn't only Mildew himself that you had to fear. And the man who made an end of him won't let any trifles stand in his way."

"It's certain he really was murdered?"

"Absolutely. There's the distance from which the bullets were fired, their direction, the fact that the shots must have been silenced, and other technical reasons.

"I'm sure of more than that, as I've told you already. I'm sure of who the murderer was. But that's not proving it. When we give the taxi driver a chance of looking at him at a distance of a few feet, and the best he'll say is that he thinks, but he can't be sure! And the maid's rather worse than that.... And when we've no possible motive that we can prove, whatever we think we know—we might put him in the dock, and it would be just asking for our resignations to be sent in.

"It's no use, in our profession, being sure of things that we can't prove. You say you're sure Mrs. Braddock had no idea of the sort of man Mildew was, and I think you're right, but could you prove that? It wouldn't be worth a try."

"Then we just throw the whole thing up, unless they murder Eustace or Mr. Catsgill or start something else fresh?"

"No, we don't. We go steadily on. We mean to put Boyle where he ought to be, and the Chief thinks that you're the one who'll be able to help in that.

"But the first essential is that he shouldn't get an idea that we're interested in him. You've got to remember that we should never have given him a thought but for Catsgill having heard his name, and that was in such a way that Mildew had no idea that he'd let it out.

"It's the end of Mildew—you might say you've done something there, for it came from what was started by you, whoever's hand fired the shot. It's the end of Mildew, but not the end of the Mildew Gang, and till they're finished you'll be one of us whose job is to hunt them down."

ABOUT THE AUTHOR

SYDNEY FOWLER WRIGHT (1874-1965) penned over seventy volumes of science fiction, fantasy, classic mysteries, historical novels, poetry, and non-fiction, many of them being published by the Borgo Press Imprint of Wildside Press.